ILLEGAL GUILT

Recent Titles by Jeffrey Ashford from Severn House

THE COST OF INNOCENCE
DEADLY CORRUPTION
EVIDENTIALLY GUILTY
FAIR EXCHANGE IS ROBBERY
AN HONEST BETRAYAL
ILLEGAL GUILT
LOOKING-GLASS JUSTICE
MURDER WILL OUT
A TRUTHFUL INJUSTICE
A WEB OF CIRCUMSTANCES

Writing as Roderic Jeffries

AN AIR OF MURDER
DEFINITELY DECEASED
AN INTRIGUING MURDER
MURDER DELAYED
MURDER NEEDS IMAGINATION
SEEING IS DECEIVING
A SUNNY DISAPPEARANCE

ILLEGAL GUILT

Jeffrey Ashford

This first world edition published in Great Britain 2007 by
SEVERN HOUSE PUBLISHERS LTD of
9–15 High Street, Sutton, Surrey SM1 1DF.
This first world edition published in the USA 2007 by
SEVERN HOUSE PUBLISHERS INC of
595 Madison Avenue, New York, N.Y. 10022.

British Library Cataloguing in Publication Data

Ashford, Jeffrey, 1926-
Illegal guilt
1. Kidnapping - Fiction 2. Police - England - Fiction
3. Detective and mystery stories
I. Title
823.9'14[F]

ISBN-13: 978-0-7278-6530-4 (cased)

Typeset by Palimpsest Book Production Ltd.,
Grangemouth, Stirlingshire, Scotland.
Printed and bound in Great Britain by
MPG Books Ltd., Bodmin, Cornwall.

One

Perry parked his car, climbed out, and crossed the yard to divisional HQ, a featureless, brick building which some years previously had replaced a sprawling, frequently altered, two-storey building which had possessed the attraction of age and unexpectedness. He went through the side door and, since the lift was out of order, climbed the stairs to the fourth floor.

The detective sergeant's door was not fully closed; he was talking loudly and aggressively over the phone. Yates was a dour, often bad-tempered man. Fuller – no respecter of age or rank; his mother was Australian – suggested that with a wife like his, the bed was always motionless and that soured the spirit. Perry continued along the corridor to the CID general room and entered. Fuller and Stone were seated at their desks. Fuller, hair scrambled, tie loose, jacket lying on the back of his chair, looked up. 'How did it go?'

'Grim.' Perry sat at his desk. 'The paramedic reckoned it was touch and go for the victim.'

'Did you find out who used the knife?'

'No problem and he's here: we're waiting for a parent to turn up so we can question him. The kid's just turned twelve. Says he's been on the wrong side of the class bully and the gang that go along with him and they've been giving him a very rough time. He tried to escape them by using a knife the size of a Bowie. Where the hell does one buy that?'

'A what?' Stone asked.

'Colonel Bowie, known for his skill with a long-bladed knife,' Fuller answered. 'Don't they teach you anything these days?'

'Sometimes they try.'

'Without success.'

Perry spoke slowly. 'It's strange . . .'

'A lot of the knives the kids carry these days are almost as big as themselves.'

'I mean, looking through the window and seeing the church and all it means when one's just back from trying to save a kid in a bloody shirt with a face the colour of chalk.'

'What's so odd about that in our job?'

'I'm talking about the contradictions in life.'

'You know your problem?'

'Tell me.'

'You think too much.'

Stone said: 'Like Cassius. Or was it Casca?'

'How's that?' Fuller demanded.

Stone seized the opportunity. 'Didn't they teach you anything in the old days?'

Perry laughed. Stone, a CID cadet, had very quickly learned to stand up for himself and not accept Fuller's supposed authority as the longest-serving detective in the room.

'Has anything come up since I've been away?' Perry enquired.

'A couple of handbag thefts, that's all. Harry's out on the job. By the way, there was a phone call for you, not long before you returned.'

'Who?'

'A woman who sounded in quite a state. Said she had to speak to you. I asked if I could help her, but she just put the receiver down.'

'My wife?' Perry asked, with immediate concern.

'I'm certain it wasn't, but for the moment I can't remember who she said she was. Had something to do with trees.'

'Very helpful.'

'That's how I remember things. It's called connective memory. It was acorn . . .'

'Mrs Acorn?'

'No. But that's close . . . Oak. Mrs Oakley.'

Perry stared out of the nearer window, his gaze unfocussed. His sister and he had not spoken to each other for a couple of years following a bitter row. After the death of his mother, his father had lived with Sandra and him. His father, normally a man who kept his opinions to himself, had, not long before his death, expressed contempt for Ray Oakley, who, he claimed, had married Elizabeth solely because her parents still owned a house with a large garden in the centre of Letstone, which obviously had potential for lucrative development. Perry had had no prior knowledge of the contents of his father's will and had been as surprised as Elizabeth had been shocked when he learned he had been left three quarters of the estate. Not long afterwards, Oakley had left Elizabeth for a widow a little older and reputedly many times richer. Perry had tried to help Elizabeth, but she had bitterly rejected his offer. She had accused him of persuading their father to alter his will to his benefit and because she had been left so proportionately little, Ray had gone off with the other woman . . .

Perry sighed. Family life could be a poisoned chalice. He crossed to the nearest desk, on which was a phone with a very long lead, carried it back to his desk, sat, and was about to dial when he realized he was uncertain of the number, which he had not used for a long time. Concentration recaptured it.

'It's Ron . . .'

'For God's sake, where have you been? I phoned hours ago,' Elizabeth said, words jostling each other.

'I've only just returned to the station. What's the problem?'

He had some difficulty in unscrambling her words. Elaine was missing. She had rung on her mobile to say Stan Burrell had been passing whilst she was waiting for the bus outside the school and he had stopped and picked her up. He would leave her by the field with the horse instead of driving her home because he had work to do. Minutes later, the phone had rung again and she'd expected the caller to be Elaine, who would say they were nearing the village. But the caller had been Madge, a gossip enthusiast, and she'd only realized how long the call had been after she'd replaced the receiver.

She had immediately driven round to the horse field. Elaine was not there and nor was the horse. She must have tried to phone home when the line was blocked. Becoming bored with no Blacky to talk to—

'Blacky?'

'The horse.'

—she had obviously decided to walk home. Yet if she had gone down to the village and along Fagg's Lane, Elizabeth would have met her in the car. The alternative and much quicker route was to walk down the dirt track through Pearce Wood, but she was forbidden to do that. So what could have happened? She must have . . .

He broke into the flow of frantically spoken words. 'Liz, was there any trouble this morning before she went to school?'

'What do you mean, trouble?'

'Did you have to tick her off over anything?'

'Only about the dog, Toby.'

'What was the problem?'

'I keep telling her she mustn't feed him titbits because

he's getting fat, but I caught her giving him some toast when she was eating breakfast. But what does that matter?'

'I need to get a picture of the morning.' As Moira, his own daughter, had taught him, youngsters could become very bolshy when corrected. Possibly Elaine's resentment had lasted right through to leaving school. That the horse was not there and she could not contact her mother would have exacerbated her resentment, perhaps to the point where she had decided to defy her mother and return through the wood. But if she had not arrived home . . . 'I'll be with you as soon as I can be.'

He replaced the receiver. Even as a child, Elizabeth had been easily panicked and according to a mutual friend, recently she had become the most possessive of mothers. Probably, Elaine would soon return, none the worse. But there always had to be the possibility she would not. He stood.

'Something up?' Stone asked.

'Could be,' he answered vaguely. He left, walked the short distance to the detective sergeant's room, stepped inside.

Yates, Fuller had suggested, had a face that looked hurriedly slapped together by an incompetent sculptor. 'Sarge, a Mrs Oakley has rung in to say her young daughter has gone missing.' He gave no indication he knew Mrs Oakley. It was an immutable rule that an officer did not work on a case in which a close relative or friend was concerned.

'How old is the kid?'

'About seven.'

'How long has she been missing?'

'An hour, give or take.'

'The facts?'

Perry began to give them.

'Why would she bother to ring to say she was nearing the village?'

'So that Mrs Oakley would be in the car, waiting by the horse.'

'What horse?'

'I gather it's usually in a field not far from the house and her daughter often talks to it.'

'Neighing?'

Perry dutifully smiled. 'Young girls are often mad keen on horses.'

'Just mad. Then what?'

'When the phone call was over, Mrs Oakley realized she was late and drove quickly to the meeting point, but there was no sign of Elaine. Since the field was empty, she judged her daughter had become bored and in a spirit of rebellion – there'd been a small row in the morning – decided to walk home through the wood, even though this had been strictly forbidden. The walk should not have taken long.'

'The kid's probably still there, picking primroses.'

'There won't be many of those around at this time of year.'

'You know what I mean,' Yates said, bad temperedly. 'But I suppose we'd best send someone along. Ask the duty sergeant to send a WPC.' In his opinion, women police officers were of little use.

'It might be an idea if I went.'

'Why?'

'It could be a nasty one, Sarge. The girl was bored and maybe feeling bloody-minded because of the morning row; if she did start to walk home, she's a long time adrift.'

Yates drummed on the desk with the fingers of his right hand. 'All right. But don't spend the rest of the day talking to the horse.'

Two

The hamlet of Beacon Cross – there was no record of a beacon ever having been built, nor could anyone suggest why one should have been – was set around crossroads. There was one house that had been a general store before supermarkets strangled almost all village shops; one house that had once been a pub before tougher drink-and-drive laws had strangled most country pubs; two other houses and a bungalow.

The crossroads were clear and Perry drove across, then first left. On one side was a neglected orchard with trees overgrown and crooked, providing a visual pleasure which no modern, commercial orchard could; on the other side, green fields surrounded a seventeenth-century timber-framed, peg-tiled farmhouse. The kind of house Elizabeth had had to give up when her husband left her for another woman. Now, she lived in a square, pebble-dashed, slate-tiled house which would not have looked out of place in a down-market coastal town.

He turned up the slightly rising lane, parked in front of Tippens Cottage. As he pushed back the squeaky gate and stepped into the garden, the front door opened and a small, cocky, pugnacious Border terrier rushed out and barked until it recognized him, then came forward to be patted.

Elizabeth appeared in the doorway. 'Have you found her?' she asked wildly.

'There's not been time to—'

'She's been kidnapped and God knows what's happening to her.'

'Liz, try to calm it.'

'Be calm when Elaine's missing?'

'I have to know the answers to some questions and you must be calm if you're to tell me what I need to know.' Her eyes were seeing imagined horrors, the lines in her face had deepened, her mouth was drawn; she looked considerably older than when he had last seen her. 'Let's go inside.'

She did not immediately move.

'The sooner I know the facts, the quicker we'll find Elaine. He moved forward, which caused her to go back and allow him to enter.

She led the way into the small front room. The untidiness convinced him she had not cleaned it for days so it had been like this before Elaine had gone missing. Depression or an inability to come to terms with the present? Was there a difference? Not a happy home for Elaine. In such circumstances, there were times when children might fantasize that if they left, they would find happiness somewhere else . . .

'Why aren't you already looking for her?' she demanded as she stood in front of the open fireplace.

He did not answer that there would be no search until it was determined Elaine really was missing and this was not a false alarm. Toby jumped up on to the settee where Perry sat and started to sniff his coat.

'Get down,' she said.

Being a terrier, Toby ignored the order and wagged his tail.

'I said, get down!' Her voice was raised.

'It's all right, Liz, he's just finding out what other dogs I've met.' He stroked Toby. 'Until recently, we had a what's-it, rescued by the RSPCA. Sadly, she died recently. Moira keeps asking us to get another dog, but it's such an emotional disaster when one dies, especially for a kid, that one hesitates. She used to dress Snatch up, much to the dog's disgust. She was called Snatch because the first day we had her, she snatched some bacon off the kitchen table and gulped it down.' He had hoped 'normal' conversation would help her to distance herself from her worst fears, but it did not.

'You've got to find her.' She walked over to an armchair and slumped down on it.

'We will.'

'By sitting there as if you don't give a damn?'

Victims seldom understood there had to be a methodical investigation, not a knee-jerk reaction to events. 'Have you tried to ring Elaine on her mobile?'

She stared at him, surprised and then shocked by her omission. She stood, rushed across to the far end of the room where the telephone stood on the small occasional table which had come from their parents' home. He watched her dial. Her hand was shaking. It was not difficult to imagine her sudden hope. Elaine would put at rest all her tortured fears . . .

She held the receiver to her ear for minutes, then replaced it. 'There's no answer,' she said dully. She returned to the chair. 'Where can she be? Where?'

'We'll find out.' He was chillingly aware of the ambiguity of his assurance. 'Did you speak to your friend, Stan Burrell?' He had to repeat the question before she could concentrate on what he had said.

'I phoned him. He said he dropped her where he sometimes does.'

'Which is where?'

'Opposite the wood. By the field where Blacky is.'

'Blacky?'

'The horse she rides.'

'Right – sorry, I did know that. What we need to do now, Liz, is go up and look at her bedroom.'

'Why?'

'To find out if any of her clothes are missing.'

'Why should they be?'

'Sometimes a daughter is sufficiently resentful when her mother ticks her off to decide to leave home, as much to punish her mother as to find a mythical somewhere where people are more understanding.'

She stood, led the way through the hall and up steep stairs. The bedroom was small and overcrowded with horse posters, model horses of all shapes, sizes, and breeds, and three large, framed photographs of Elaine on a horse. He had forgotten how attractive she was, not having seen her since a casual meeting in Carnford, which had been cut short by Elizabeth. Curly auburn hair spilled out from under a hard hat, her eyes were deep blue, mouth firm and shapely, chin rounded; a suggestion of youthful gamin added character.

'Do you remember what she was wearing when she left this morning?' he asked.

'Of course I do.'

'Then look through her clothes and see if you reckon any are missing.'

She examined the dresses, shirts, and skirts hanging in the cupboard, the clothes in the chest of drawers. 'There's nothing gone.'

He pointed to a large, ragged model horse by the side of the pillows, swathed in a tatty blue blanket. 'Is that her blue?'

When young, Elizabeth had carried a blue knitted doll's blanket everywhere; had taken it to bed and fallen asleep gripping the satin edging.

'I suppose it is,' she answered, her mind not on what she said.

'Does she have any money?'

'I've made her save some of what she's been given as presents.'

'Could she draw that on her own?'

'I keep the pass book.'

'And you still have it?'

'Of course I do.'

She had failed to see the significance of that or of the presence of the blanket on the bed.

'Let's go back downstairs.'

Once they were seated, he said, 'Stan Burrell drove her back from school: will you tell me something about him?'

'Why?'

'Does he live locally?'

'Yes.'

'What does he do in life?'

'He's a farmer.'

'What age?'

'What the hell does all this matter?'

'Just accept it does and bear with me. How old is he?'

'I suppose he's about forty-five, fifty.'

'How did you come to meet him?'

She looked as if she was again about to demand why he was asking stupid questions, but finally answered. 'Soon after we'd moved here, Elaine was talking to Blacky. Stan saw her and chatted, asked if she'd like to ride Blacky. She . . .' She stopped.

'Yes?'

'She rushed home to tell me what had happened. She was so excited, she started dancing around the place. Banged into the cabinet over there and cracked the glass. I was annoyed because it had come from our old home and that made her upset . . . But then she remembered about the horse and was cheerful and told me what a wonderful horse Blacky was and how she'd train him to do everything . . .' Her thoughts drifted back to the past.

'Why does Burrell sometimes pick Elaine up from school?'

'Why can't you stop asking questions?'

'They're important, Liz.'

'He picks her up because it saves waiting for the bus.'

'Is he married?'

'No.'

'Interested in women?'

'How the hell would I know?'

'Do you ever see him with a woman?'

'No . . . There's gossip he was once engaged to someone, but she upped and left him.'

'Do you like him?'

'He's been very kind to Elaine, letting her ride Blacky whenever she wants. It helped her get over leaving Tredgarth and all her friends.'

'Would you call him a close friend?'

'No.'

'Does he know Elaine's not come back?'

'I phoned him and said she hadn't. I told you.'

'Of course you did. What exactly did he tell you?'

'That he'd left her by the horse field because he had needed to get a load of hay in before it rained. Yet if he'd known there was the slightest chance of what might happen, he would have driven her right back and never mind the hay . . . It wouldn't have taken him long . . . Not more than five minutes . . .' She gripped her hands together and tightened her fingers until they whitened.

'Why d'you think he has been so kind to her?'

'Why not?' She unclasped her fingers. 'When are you going to do something instead of sitting there?' she asked shrilly.

'Liz, right now, your answers are more important than

anything else. Have you ever been worried by his kindness to Elaine?'

'Because he might be trying to fool with her? You reckon if I'd thought that, I'd have let her within a mile of him?'

'She's never mentioned anything which disturbed you, even briefly?'

'What sort of a mother would I be if she had, yet I continued to let her see him?'

'A mother can believe her child is making an incident up.'

'If she'd told me about anything of the sort you're suggesting, I'd have believed her and made certain she was never with him again.'

He stood. 'I need to walk through Pearce Wood.'

'Then I'm coming with you.'

'No.'

'You think she's there, don't you?'

'No, I don't. I need to know how long it would take to walk from the road to here.'

'Why?'

'One of the burdens of my job is I have to confirm everything, even if it's of little account. And I need to be on my own to concentrate, which I won't be able to do if you're with me.'

It was a weak explanation, but she accepted it.

He left the house, walked up the lane, which bore left to skirt the small wood. By the entrance of a central bridle path through the wood was the sign 'No trespassing', on which, in spray paint, had been added another prohibition of a different nature.

He entered the wood, walked slowly up the path. It had been coppiced only a few years before and ash, hornbeam, birch, beech, oak, chestnut were growing freely, but brambles, bracken, and occasional rhododendron bushes, still provided ground cover.

He reached the edge of the wood, stepped out on to the grass verge bordering Clees Road. Opposite was an empty field down to grass with corral fencing – presumably where the horse was usually kept. To the right, hay, late as was most that year in contrast to the early harvest, was being tedded; to the left, sheep were grazing. A pastoral scene to please any country-lover unless he was wondering if it might be hiding his niece who had been raped and perhaps murdered.

He retraced his steps and when halfway down the path, stopped, brought out his mobile from his pocket, dialled Tippens Cottage.

'Yes?' said Elizabeth, breathless from having rushed to answer the call.

'It's Ron.'

'Oh! I thought . . .' Her bitter disappointment was obvious.

'I want you to try again to contact Elaine on her mobile.'

Disappointment was replaced with hope. 'You think she'll answer this time? You know where she is?'

'It's an experiment.'

'But—'

'Just do it, Liz.' He cut the connection before she could ask more questions.

He waited. A pigeon flew in, intending to land on an ash, but saw him at the last moment and fled with a clatter of wings; a scampering sound identified a grey squirrel running across the ground to reach a chestnut sapling.

The few bars of a tune he did not recognize sounded to his right; at a guess, from a clump of brambles.

He phoned Yates to report that a search team was needed in Pearce Wood.

Three

Detective Inspector Clark was intelligent, resourceful, and a hard worker, but perhaps lucky to have reached his present rank and unlikely to gain further promotion. A successful detective was occasionally faced with a case which called for an imaginative approach to rules and regulations and an understanding that justice and the law could disagree if he were to succeed in solving it. For Clark, imagination could be dangerous; the law *was* justice; rules and regulations were carved in stone.

He had a solid figure, a well proportioned face, unusually long and shapely fingers which had made his grandmother, a woman of some irrationality, believe he should become a concert pianist. He dressed more carefully than many and often sported a rose in his lapel, a fact that always caused amused scorn among the rank and file. They believed it to be typical of his wife to send him out looking like a Boulevard Bertie. They disliked her because when there was occasion to meet her, she made it clear she was the wife of their superior officer. She would have made a good admiral's spouse.

DI Clark left his car and crossed briskly to where Perry waited, together with several men in uniform. 'Give me a rundown.'

Perry spoke concisely. The DI liked unadorned facts.

'Show me where the mobile sounds off.' He turned and spoke to the uniform sergeant. 'Stay here until you're called.'

The sergeant acknowledged the order.

'Would you like to start moving since we don't want to be here all night,' Clark said.

If he'd moved before, that would have been wrong, Perry thought. He began to walk down the path.

'Is this track used a lot?' Clark asked abruptly.

'I can't say for certain, sir.'

'We'll need to know.'

In other words, he should have had the initiative to find out. Moments later, he came to a halt. 'The mobile is on a line with here, sir; perhaps in those brambles.'

'Phone it.'

By good judgment, he had called Elizabeth a second time and asked for the number of Elaine's mobile. He dialled it on his mobile and the thin, reedy notes of the unrecognized tune sounded.

'You're right,' Clark said. 'It's in those brambles.'

One couldn't be wrong all the time.

'We'll go back up.'

They returned to the road. The men were lined up and the search began. Using sticks to part the undergrowth, they moved slowly down the gently sloping land to the accompaniment of the shouts of the sergeant, demanding they maintain the line. When closing on the brambles from which it was judged the phone had sounded, they were halted.

Clark moved forward towards the clump of tightly entwined bramble trails, then circled it, visually searching for depressed or crushed foliage which would indicate the passage of someone. He returned and spoke to Perry. 'There are no signs of anyone walking there so probably the mobile was thrown, not dropped. Tell SOCO to go forward and retrieve it.'

The scene of crime officer, not wearing plastic overalls or shoe covers because of conditions, left the line and, moving even more slowly than had the DI, went forward. Having reached the clump, he circled it, studying the ground, then repeated the movement using a stick to examine the interior of the clump. He finally enlarged an opening, put the stick down on the ground, pulled on plastic gloves, checked his balance, and reached into the centre of the clump, swearing as he did so when a thorn gouged the side of his wrist, having pierced his glove. He brought out a mobile, which he dropped into an exhibits bag, checked there was nothing else of interest, returned to where Clark stood, and showed him the mobile.

'Is that the model and make of phone the girl was carrying?' Clark asked.

In the rush, that was something Perry had not remembered to find out, but since it would not have answered the call had it not been Elaine's, he confirmed that it was.

The SOCO finished recording on the label of the exhibits bag the location, time, date, and his identity.

Clark gave the order to continue searching.

They reached the end of the wood, turned and regrouped to search the second half. Within a couple of minutes, there was a shout that something had been found.

Clark hurried across to where a PC, some fifteen feet in from the path, pointed to one of the shoots growing from a hornbeam bole; a twig had been broken off and on the remaining stub had been caught a thread of light blue cotton.

'Smart sighting,' Clark said.

The PC hid his surprise. Clark was noted for his readiness to criticize, not praise.

Perry was called across. 'You have a full description of what the child was wearing?' Clark asked.

'Vest, pants, frock, socks, and shoes. Her mother described her dress as light blue.'

Clark called the SOCO across. 'Cut the twig close to the stem.'

The constable opened out a penknife and prepared to cut the twig.

'Lower,' Clark ordered.

He took a long time to judge where to cut, suggesting he considered the order unnecessary. The twig, with thread attached, was dropped into an exhibits bag, on which were noted the usual details.

As the light under the trees was beginning to fade, the search was concluded. The men made their way to the cars and van.

'I want tape around the areas where the mobile and thread were found,' Clark said.

Someone groaned.

He spoke to Perry. 'Show the thread to Mrs Oakley and find out if she can confirm it came from her daughter's dress.'

Crime so often injured many more people than the initial victim. He crossed to the van where the SOCO was about to climb into the back. 'Hang on, George.'

'Why?'

'I need the thread to show the mother for identification.'

The other stepped back from the van. 'Sooner you than me, that's for sure. Be like telling a wife her husband's just driven into a wall at sixty. She'll not be sleeping well tonight . . . Sign.'

Perry wrote in the exhibits record book that exhibit No. 2, case 153/3, had been handed to him by SOCO Smelland, thus ensuring the continuity of evidence was maintained. No smart-arsed lawyer would be able to claim in court that the evidence had been tampered with.

He returned to where Clark stood. 'I have the thread, sir.' He indicated the bag in his right hand. He turned to leave.

'Accepting the facts, Perry, what's your interpretation of them?'

He was surprised to be asked since the DI so seldom welcomed others' judgments. 'Elaine was dropped across the road, by the horse field. She waited for her mother, who didn't turn up because she'd lost track of time. Becoming bored with no horse to talk to, resentful her mother wasn't there and because of the row that morning, she decided to do what she had been forbidden to do and started to return home through the wood. Someone, and it has to be all but certain it was a man, followed her. Frightened, she tried to phone for help, but he grabbed the mobile out of her hand and threw it away. In doing this, he had only one hand holding her and she was able to break free and run. Unfortunately, he caught her and there was a struggle during which her frock was caught on the twig.'

'Until something more turns up, that seems to be the most likely scenario. What was the man's motive?'

'Rape.'

'Probably. If the ground were not so hard, we might have found evidence of this. If he did not kill her to prevent identification, she would have made her way home or, if too injured, we would have found her. If he did kill her, we would have found the body unless he carried that away to hide it where it would be likely to remain until too decayed to offer any meaningful evidence. At daylight tomorrow, a search of other woods in the area must be carried out.

'We have to consider the possibility of kidnapping for sex at his leisure or for profit. Is the family wealthy enough to be good for a large ransom?'

'Far from it.'

'Does the father work in a job that places him in possession of information which could be put to political or financial use by an abductor who would use the child to blackmail him into handing it over?'

'Her father left home and family some time ago and took off with another woman. He worked in the Department of Social Services.'

'You're very conversant with the family history,' Clark observed.

Perry hastened to explain to prevent Clark envisaging the possibility of relationship. 'Mrs Oakley was in a very emotional state when I spoke to her and she told me a great deal about the family without really realizing what she was saying.'

'It won't help asking her if she can identify the thread, but it has to be done. If she does identify it, give me a bell at the station.'

'Right, sir.'

'And get confirmation Burrell did drop Elaine by the woods.'

'He assured Mrs Oakley he did.'

'I want confirmation that's given by him to you, not to a third party.'

Doubting Thomas Clark, Perry thought bitterly.

Four

Perry's visit was as emotionally disturbing as he had feared. As Toby jumped up, demanding attention, Elizabeth stared at the blue thread on the twig inside the plastic bag.

'Is that the colour of the dress Elaine was wearing?' he asked. 'Is the material the same as far as you can tell?'

She did not answer.

'I have to know, Liz.'

'Where . . .'

'We found it in the woods.'

'You can't have done.'

'We did.'

'You can't. She was told never to walk in them on her own.'

'Is that from her dress?'

She made small whimpering sounds which disturbed Toby and reminded Perry of his horror, when young, of hearing the cries of a rabbit caught in an illegal gin trap. He went forward and put his arms around her. He felt her stiffen and thought that even the harrowing present would not allow her to forget the past, then she relaxed and clung to him.

'It's . . . oh, God, it's her dress.'

Fifteen minutes later, he left the house, settled in the car, used the mobile to phone Clark. 'Mrs Oakley says the thread is the same colour and consistency as the dress Elaine was wearing.'

'Have you spoken to Burrell?'

'I'm on my way now.'

'Keep me posted.'

He started the engine, looked at the time. Sandra would have cause once again to consider what poor husbands policemen made. Their faults were many. They bonded too firmly, drank heavily, met women who offered a quickie for a favour, were regarded with reservation by neighbours which made it difficult for the wives to form local friendships, and could never, ever be trusted to return home on time.

In his room in divisional HQ, Clark rang county HQ. 'Can I speak to Superintendent Woolley?'

He was told to wait. Typical! He disliked Woolley, yet would have scorned the suggestion that much of this dislike was due to jealousy. They had joined the force within days of each other, had trained together at the newly instituted police college, had left with good records and the prospect of frequent promotion. Woolley had enjoyed this, he had not. Woolley was large, gregarious, quick to gain friendship.

'What is it?' Woolley asked abruptly.

'Inspector Clark here, sir.' That 'sir' was unwelcome.

'Well?'

No friendly comment, no reference to past times at the college, no 'How are things, Harry?'

'We have a missing girl and it's beginning to look nasty.'

'The facts?'

He made his report brief because Woolley disliked official prolixity. Yet he would take minutes to tell a poor joke and then laugh loud and long.

'You've called a press meeting to get the facts on the screen and in the papers?'

'That's why I'm ringing now. I need your permission to contact the media.'

'Why didn't you do that before asking?' The line went dead.

Clark replaced the receiver. How did one respect a senior who believed rules were to be ignored?

Perry drove along the straight road to the low hill on which Rickton stood and at the base of which was Morning Farm. He had not recognized the address, but as he picked out the farm in the gathering gloom, he remembered it and that on first noting it he had renamed it Midnight Farm. He turned off the road and into the yard. As the headlights swept round, they picked out dilapidated outbuildings; an ancient Ferguson tractor – a museum piece; several other implements of equal vintage; a shed that leaned over and around the pop-hole of which were a couple of chickens; several cows of indeterminate breed lackadaisically chewing the cud; a pigpen made from wooden sleepers; two Dutch barns constructed from telegraph poles and corrugated iron, the first of which was filled with hay, the second with a few feet of sheaves of corn. By the corner of the second barn was the largest Rottweiler he had ever seen, chained to a kennel. He braked to a halt immediately past the barns, by the side of a white van in a condition which made him think it must have evaded road testing.

As he climbed out of the car, the Rottweiler barked and snarled as it strained at its chain. Understudy for the Hound of the Baskervilles. Two powerful, unshaded lights on the outside of the house were switched on; the front door opened, Burrell stepped out on to the top flagstone step.

If, Perry decided as he walked towards the house, this place was reminiscent of a rundown farm during the Depression, Burrell epitomized the farmer of that time. Powerfully built, deep lines in his face which marked the sullenness of failure, uncut hair, stubble, and clothing, showed a complete lack of self-esteem. Had he not offered Elaine riding, would Elizabeth have thought twice before refusing to allow Elaine to be in his company? 'Mr Stanley Burrell?'

'What of it?' he asked harshly.

'Detective Constable Perry, local CID.'

Burrell shouted at the dog to shut up.

'You don't want unannounced visitors,' Perry said lightly.

'What's it to you?'

He had tried to make the meeting initially pleasant, yet to judge from his manner, Burrell already seemed threatened. 'Just praising your canine alarm system.'

'It's the pikies. Always trying to pinch something.'

'I imagine that now they leave you severely alone . . . You've heard Elaine Oakley is missing?'

'Her mum phoned.'

'I'm wondering if you can in any way help me find out where she might be?'

Burrell said quickly, 'Don't know nothing.'

'You may think that, but . . .'

'I ain't seen her since I left her at the field.'

'Do you think I might come inside so that we can talk without trying to outshout the dog?'

Burrell gave no answer, returned indoors. Perry crossed to the flagstone steps, climbed them and went inside. He had expected the interior of the house to be in the same state of neglect as was the farm outside, but the large beamed sitting room, with inglenook fireplace, was clean and tidy and on an occasional table was a vase in which were several red roses in early bloom. It was a reasonable guess that a daily did the housework.

Burrell slumped down in an ancient chair, Perry sat on another and immediately noticed the lack of springing. He spoke pleasantly. 'What I'd like you to tell me is what happened from the moment you picked up Elaine outside the school.'

'Nothing happened.'

'Let's start at the beginning. You saw her waiting for the bus outside her school. Does that occur often?'

'She needs to get home, don't she?'

'You misunderstand me. Do you often pick her up at the bus stop?'

'When I sees her.'

'How often would that be?'

'Can't say.'

'Do you frequently drive into Carnford?'

'Depends.'

'On what?'

'Whether I need something.'

Perry spoke lightly. 'That's logical! So what was the problem that took you into Carnford this time?'

'Needed something for the harvester.'

'You were cutting corn and it broke down?'

'Wouldn't of needed something if it hadn't.'

'And when you'd brought back the part you needed, what did you do?'

'Drove back.'

'I'm becoming a little confused. I understood you told Mrs Oakley how sorry you were because you'd been unable to drive Elaine home since you had to carry hay before the weather broke.'

'Harvesting, loading, teddering – what's it matter?'

'It doesn't. Just me, trying to get things dead right because I've a boss who wants everything exact . . . You saw Elaine in Carnford, waiting for the bus, so you picked her up and drove her back to Beacon Cross. You were in a hurry to return to work, so you told her you'd have to leave her by the horse field?'

'Yes.'

'Did you say the horse wasn't in the field?'

'Can't remember.'

'Bear with me, Mr Burrell. I find this as irritating as you do and I'm trying to keep things short. Why wasn't the horse there?'

'Why d'you think?'

'If I knew anything about horses, I might be able to answer.'

'It needed fresh pasture.'

'Does that often happen?'

'Depends how quick the grass grows or the land gets mucked.'

'How many seats are there in your van?'

The change of subject mentally bewildered Burrell. Perry repeated the question.

'Are you daft, asking that?'

'Probably slightly unhinged after several years in the job. Are there seats in the rear?'

'Don't you listen? Ain't you seen it outside? I use it to carry pellets, crushed barley, not people.'

'Then Elaine was sitting by your side?'

'You reckon I'd put her in with the sacks?'

'She always phoned her mother on her mobile as she approached Beacon Cross, didn't she?'

Burrell grunted an answer.

'You gathered she couldn't get through to her mother this afternoon?'

'How was I to know that?'

'You weren't aware she used her mobile to phone home and tried more than once without success?'

'No.'

'You didn't notice her punching in the numbers?'

'What's that bloody got to do with the kid? And when I'm driving, I watch the road, not what someone else is doing.'

'She didn't say anything, didn't mutter her annoyance?'

'No.'

'When you arrived at the horse field, it was clear her mother was not there to meet her. Yet you left her. Why?'

'Reckoned her mum would be along.'

'You weren't worried about leaving her there?'

'Spends enough time on her own with the horse.'

'It didn't occur to you that since the horse wasn't there, she might get quickly bored and return home?'

'Where's the problem? Kids are around the roads all the time in daylight.'

'Had she mentioned to you there'd been a row with her mother in the morning?'

'No.'

'Did you get any impression that she was in a bit of a bolshy mood?'

'No.'

'So it didn't occur to you that she might decide to return home through the woods in a gesture of childish defiance?'

'Here, are you trying to blame me for her being missing? Because if you are, you don't know bleeding nothing. I like the kid and wouldn't never touch her.'

'What exactly do you mean by "touch her"?'

'You know.'

Perry stood. 'One last question, do you get your spares for machinery from Old George's yard?'

'What if I does?'

'Just wondered. Thanks for your help.'

As he stepped out on to the first flagstone, the Rottweiler began to bark and snarl. As he walked to his car, he decided he should have asked Burrell how long he had had the dog.

Five

Neighbours complained bitterly that the two acres around the house on the edge of Carnford were an appalling eyesore, but Old George – Young George since his father had died – perversely continued to enlarge the junkyard since it was becoming more and more profitable as the desire to restore houses, old vehicles, and machinery increased. Amidst the apparent disorder were broken-down cars; ancient farm implements; tiles; beams; doors; bricks; shaped ragstone; fireplaces; windows; dismantled barns; even a steam engine which, uniquely, was well looked after and had its brass polished.

Perry parked under a tall street light, crossed the pavement and, since there was no bell, hammered on the wooden gates, which were reinforced with bands of rusting steel.

Eventually, there was an angry shout telling him to eff off or the police would be called.

'They're already here. CID.'

After a while, one gate was slowly swung open.

Perry stepped inside. The chaos to the right of, and beyond, the house was largely in half dark, and this and the shadows turned it into a scene of formless destruction. Life after a Martian invasion.

'You know what the effing time is?' Young George demanded.

'Long after since I should have been in bed, warming my feet on the missus.'

'Then clear off and warm 'em.'

'You expect me to forget a snout's given us the buzz that there's fifty kilos of smack just been delivered here?'

Young George stepped out on to the pavement and looked to his left and right. 'You ain't heard nothing or there'd be a bloody army of you waiting.'

'Maybe they'll be along later. Still, since I'm here, you can answer a question or two before you get back to counting up your profits.'

'Profits? With this government stealing everything the rest of us earn?'

'That's what governments are for. Do you know Stan Burrell?'

'I've maybe seen him.'

'Lighten up.'

'Comes in sometimes, wanting bits for his machinery what ought to've been thrown out years ago.'

'But since none of it has been, he must be a profitable customer.'

'Him? He's so tight, if he'd ever had a father, he'd of let him starve rather than buy him any grub.'

'How often does he come here?'

'When he has to.'

'When was he last here?'

'How would I remember?'

'By trying.'

After a while, Young George said, 'Three, four weeks ago; needed a chain for his baler. Found him one and he started saying it wasn't worth what I was asking.'

'Sensible man.'

'I told him, if it ain't worth it to you, try elsewhere. Didn't shut him up. He'd haggle with the devil. Bought some hay last year from a local farmer and argued the price so hard, the other bloke near gave it to him.'

'You've not seen him in weeks?'

'Like I said.'

'Could he have come here for a part for his thresher in the past day or two without you knowing he had?'

'You reckon I scrape a living by letting people swindle me when I'm looking the other way?'

'Seems highly unlikely. OK, thanks for your help.'

'You try to batter down me gates in the middle of the night just to ask me when I last saw him?'

'That's the picture.'

'So what if I wake you in the middle of the bloody night to ask the time?'

'I'll arrest you.'

Almost every window in divisional HQ was lit when Perry drove into the courtyard and parked in the bay marked Chief Inspector since it was near the entrance. He entered and as he made for the stairs heard a teenager drunkenly protesting that he was sober and had not been exposing himself in the High Street.

The DI, looking as exhausted as Perry felt, was leaning back in his chair and resting the phone receiver between ear and shoulder as he listened to a one-sided call. He spoke a few words, replaced the receiver. 'D division will start searching other woods at daybreak.'

'That'll take them all day, maybe some of the night as well.'

'Probably. What's your story?'

'Burrell is sticking to what he's said previously, but he made one or two interesting changes and one or two questionable statements.'

'Grab a seat and tell me.'

Perry carried a chair from against the wall and set it down in front of the desk. He described his questioning of Burrell and his brief visit to Young George's junkyard.

'Are you spotting Burrell?' Clark asked.

'It's difficult to accept he wasn't aware that Elaine

couldn't get through to home on her mobile. He says he can't remember whether he told her the horse wasn't in the field when one would imagine the first thing she asked after getting in the van was how was the horse. Then I don't remember a weather forecast of rain, yet he told Mrs Oakley he couldn't drive Elaine all the way home because he had to rush to carry hay before the weather broke. He told me he'd been in to Carnford in the afternoon to find a spare for his thresher, yet Young George reckons he'd not been near the yard. Another thing, with no prompting, Burrell told me he'd never touched Elaine. Guilt causing a denial before there was any accusation?'

'Not necessarily.'

'Sir, if I asked you if you'd been in a vehicle with a young girl sitting next to you, would you rush to tell me you hadn't touched her?'

'These days, maybe. Take a photo of your two-year-old daughter in the bath and you'll find yourself suspected of child pornography.'

'He was just too quick to deny what hadn't been alleged.'

'Is he on the sex offenders' list?'

'I haven't been able to check that yet.'

'As soon as you can.' Clark leaned forward and rested his elbows on the desk. 'The facts you've just given me aren't evidence.'

'Surely they provide an indication – and a pretty strong one at that?'

'Perhaps. Yet it's best not to forget that Elaine's mother allowed her to be picked up at school and driven home by him. That says she has no suspicions of the man and a mother's judgment is usually spot on.'

'Elaine's crazy about horses and Burrell offered her the chance of limitless riding. It's not impossible that Mrs Oakley, realizing how much that would mean to Elaine and how it would make up for the move and the loss of old friends, did not judge as firmly as she should have done. And a clever man can create a false impression of himself.'

'You would rate him clever?'

'Perhaps I should have said cunning.'

'You are not suggesting, I imagine, that we are justified in taking any action as yet?'

'When a young girl's life is at terrible risk, sir, there is sufficient reason to question Burrell again and to search his farm.'

'You don't think that perhaps you are allowing emotion to overcome rational judgment?'

'Better that than the other way around.'

'A moot point which I am not prepared to discuss at this time of night.'

'We do nothing?'

'You are well aware we are doing all we can.'

'Except apply for a search warrant.'

'Which we will not do until we have the hard evidence to support the application.' Clark picked up a pencil and revolved it between finger and thumb. After a moment, he said, 'Are you in any way, through relationship or friendship, too involved with Mrs Oakley for you to continue in this case?'

'No, sir.'

'Very well.'

Perry left.

Six

Sandra had black, curly hair, dark brown, expressive eyes, a retroussé nose, lips made for eating peaches or kissing, a dimpled chin, and a trim body through careful dieting except on high days and holidays, and when pistachio ice cream was on the menu.

'What a surprise!' she exclaimed as Perry opened the front door and stepped into the narrow hall. 'You've been missing for so long I wondered how soon I would learn I had to go into mourning. Then, low and behold, you return and I don't have to buy a black frock.'

'I'm sorry, Sandy, but—'

'I suppose you had so much to think about, you forgot Moira and I were having tea with Jean and Peter and that you had promised to turn up later for a drink. Or did the offer of one or two drinks not carry much weight in the face of a jolly at the local? Did Andy again offer the nearest blonde to perform a naked Hawaiian war dance?'

'I haven't been near a pub and—'

'Of course not. How could I have been so disloyal as to imagine my husband would engage in such jollity with the lads when he has promised by all the gods on Olympus to visit my sister and brother-in-law? Please forgive me. I should have realized your absence was beyond your control. Did the car break down yet again? We really must afford another which is more reliable. Or would you not welcome that since it wouldn't afford a reasonable excuse? No matter. You have returned before daybreak and I am not a widow so I should rejoice, not complain.' She paused, but briefly. 'And now you would no doubt like some supper – or should it be called an early breakfast?' She went into the kitchen, slammed the door shut.

About to follow and explain, he stopped when Moira said, 'I think Mummy's annoyed with you.'

'I wouldn't be surprised if you're right.' He looked up at the top floor. Moira, in a floral nightdress, was standing behind the banisters.

'She said perhaps she would become a nun. Why would she want to do that?'

'To escape the polluting presence of men.'

'Aunty Jean was upset that you didn't turn up. Do you think she would like to be a nun?'

'Married to Uncle Peter, she may well have considered the possibility.'

'I heard her say to Mummy, she wondered if you hadn't arrived because you didn't seem to like Uncle Peter.'

'You ears are too long and hear incorrectly. Aunty Jean knows how I get on very well with him. Every time he asks me how is Doctor Watson, I laugh.'

'Why do you laugh?'

'To prevent myself from committing an aggravated assault.'

'What's an aggravated assault?'

'Worse than a simple assault.'

'I don't understand what you're talking about.'

'Don't bother. It's unimportant.'

'Why didn't you come to the party?'

'Because—'

'Because your father forgot all about the invitation and his solemn promise,' Sandra said, as she came out of the kitchen.

'Why did he?'

'Because he has an accommodating memory.'

'What's that?'

'One that forgets what it doesn't wish to remember. Now, young lady, what are you doing up at this ungodly hour?'

'I woke up and heard Daddy talking.'

'A rude awakening. Back to sleep.'

He watched Sandra climb the stairs and lead Moira back into the end bedroom, then went through to the kitchen. Sandra enjoyed cooking and only served meals from a supermarket's deepfreeze when absolutely necessary. The smell emanating from the oven sharpened his hunger. But first a drink. He crossed to the small larder, picked up a can of lager, pulled the tab free, drank.

Sandra hurried into the kitchen, came to a stop and stared at him. 'Are you keeping the home fires burning?'

'Wouldn't it more logically be, putting them out? Sandra, I—'

'Jean particularly wanted you to meet her cousin and family who have been living in Canada for the past years. She said you and the husband would have so much in common. Perhaps that was her way of suggesting he also thinks only of himself.'

'I had to—'

'There's no need to think up some convoluted excuse for your behaviour. After so many years of suffering it, I've grown accustomed – or should I say, resigned? – to it. After all, look what's happened recently. We were going to that film that won an Oscar and I so wanted to see; Pat had even arrived to look after Moira when you rang and called off. Then last month we were going to celebrate my birthday and see a show in London, but you suddenly had to work late. I'm surprised that I've never thought to wonder whether the attraction is a blonde or brunette, but I suppose I'm trusting. And, of course, like all men, if you were having an affair, you would have been offering over-elaborate excuses, not the same dull one of duty calling. Of course, I do enjoy a compensation. Every time you let me down, I know this is because you are helping the community and what could be more worthwhile than that, even if at the expense of the family.'

'I told you before we were married that my job was likely to make things difficult for you from time to time.'

'I would prefer to say, all the time. Jean asked if you hadn't turned up because our marriage was becoming rocky. She has such a jealous nature and would love to think my marriage is as disastrous as was her first one.'

'Liz phoned to say she was in terrible trouble—'

'So naturally, as a dutiful brother, you had to rush to help her, even if at the expense of not keeping your promise to your wife. Had she lost something? Toby's collar?'

'She told me Ellie was missing.'

She stared at him, her anger vanishing. 'How missing?'

'She hadn't returned home from school.'

'But she has since?'

'No.'

'Then what in the hell's happened?'

'After leaving school, she waited for a bus; someone she knew saw her, picked her up, and dropped her opposite Pearce Wood. Liz had forbidden her to go through the wood, but it seems she must have started to do so. She never arrived home. We've searched, questioned people, done everything we could. Frankly, in the turmoil, I did forget your sister and to let you know what was going on.'

She came forward and put her arms around him, rested her cheek against his. 'I've been a real bitch of a wife. Will you forgive me?'

'I've forgotten what there is to forgive.'

She freed herself. 'What's happening now?'

'The search of nearby woods will continue when it's

daylight, any local person on the sex offenders' list will be questioned; the usual.'

'Christ! You think she's been taken by a pervert?'

'We found her mobile in the woods and a thread from her dress which had become snagged on a twig. It's difficult to reckon that what happened was anything other than that a man accosted her, she ran, he caught her and carried her off.'

'How can there be such vile people?'

'Someone wrote that the human capacity for tenderness is limited; for violence, limitless.'

'She could be suffering—'

He interrupted her for a change. 'Best not to imagine.'

'How can one not do so?'

'I wish I knew. Look, love, I've got to get some shut-eye before I return to the station by daybreak. Can I have some grub quickly?'

'Of course, but . . .'

'You're surprised I want to eat after what's happened? My eating means I'm hungry, not indifferent.'

'It's just . . .'

'I know.'

Seven

The early daylight accentuated the formless fronts of the terrace houses in Effington Road. Built soon after the First World War, they had cost £300 each; now they sold for tens of thousands. Most were well maintained, some had colourful window boxes, a very few showed signs of neglect.

Perry rang the bell of No. 17. When there was no response, he pressed it continuously. An upstairs window was opened. 'What's the bleeding problem?' a man shouted.

'CID.'

After a pause, he said, with affected and absurd gentility, 'Sorry about my greeting, but it is very early.'

'Not too early to knock the door in, so belt up and open up.'

The front door, its paint peeling, was opened and Hyde, tall, thin, a characterless face, dressed in a black silk dressing gown with red dragons over bright green pyjamas, stood in the doorway. 'It's Mr Parry if I remember correctly,' he said with soapy deference.

'You don't. It's Perry.'

'My humble apologies for so socially egregious a mistake. There is some way in which I might be able to help you?'

'In which you will.' One could regard Hyde with sarcastic scorn until one read his criminal record; then there could be only angry contempt.

'Please to enter my humble abode, Mr Perry.'

He stepped into a dark passage which smelled of something unpleasant he could not identify.

'Shall we go in here?' Hyde opened a door to his right. 'A poor room in which to receive, yet rich in welcome.'

The room was small and over-furnished, yet immaculately clean and tidy.

'Please do sit, Mr Perry.'

'I'll stand. Where were you yesterday afternoon?'

'May I ask why my whereabouts is of interest?'

'Cut the crap.'

'Could it be because a young lady who lives in a village not far from here is missing?'

'How do you know that?'

'I watch the news, Mr Perry, as I like to remain *au courant* with the world. I believe that is the right expression?'

'What you believe would make Beelzebub shudder.'

'Your being here means that tragically she has not yet been found?'

'You don't know she hasn't?'

'You can't think I would have had any part in her disappearance!'

'It's the first thought to come to mind.'

'I swear I know nothing about her.'

'Where were you yesterday afternoon?'

'At what time?'

'The whole afternoon; miss five minutes and I'll shake them out of you.'

'I had lunch with a friend . . .'

'His name?'

'Johnny Markham. Perchance you know him?'

'I'm in luck since I don't.'

'As I said, we ate . . .'

'Where?'

'The Cockatrice. The cuisine there is superior to . . .'

'When did you leave?'

'It's difficult to say.'

'It'll be a cold cell for you if you don't.'

'I suppose the hour was progressing since we had finished eating and the waiter was making it seem he wanted us to leave.'

'He'll have been doing that from the moment you walked in. Give me a time.'

'It might have been about two.'

'Where did you go after that?'

'Johnny and me had a jar or two at the Seven Pillars. That's a pub.'

'If you hadn't told me, I'd have imagined it was a college of higher education. When did you leave?'

'Could have been three, more or less.'

'I want a shufty around the house.'

'You do have a search warrant, Mr Perry?'

'You've something to hide?'

'Of course not.'

'Then we don't need to worry about a warrant unless you're going to try to be awkward. The last bloke who did that is away on a five-year stretch.'

A twenty-minute search confirmed Elaine was not being held in the house or the small shed at the back and that there was nothing to suggest she ever had been.

The publican of the Seven Pillars was a good advertisement for his trade. Round, overweight, cheerful, and custodian of innumerable politically incorrect jokes to recall the time when there had been free speech in Britain.

'Bob Hyde? Aye, I know him. Though that's no more than by sight and a little chatting. Always thought there's something about him . . .' He looked enquiringly across the bar.

Perry ignored the unasked question. 'Is he here often?'

'Most days.'

'What about yesterday?'

'Difficult to say. I mean, with so many customers and him being a regular, it's not easy to be certain.'

'He was with a friend. Name of Johnny Markham.'

'Makes a couple with Bob, he does. Now you mention him, I remember them both coming in yesterday.'

'What time would that have been?'

'That's going to be difficult. Lil hadn't gone off duty, since she served them, and it was before I'd had a row with the cocky little bastard of a manager . . . Call it three thirty and it won't be far wrong.'

'How long did they stay here?'

'Quite a time. Say half to three quarters of an hour.'

If Hyde had been drinking there at three thirty, he had not been in Pearce Wood when Elaine started to walk through it.

It took little time to judge the impossibility of Thurston's guilt. The faded woman who looked as if life had never dealt her a higher card than a deuce, said, 'Bert ain't here.'

'So where is he?' Perry demanded roughly, accepting it was not fair to blame her for Thurston's record, yet doing so all the same.

'He's been in hospital for the last week.'

'Which one?'

'The General.'

'What's he suffering from?'

'Got knocked over by a cab. Near died, they say.'

A chance missed.

Yates was not in his room; Perry went along to the DI's. Clark looked drained of energy.

'Yes?'

'I'm just back, sir, from questioning—' The external telephone interrupted him.

Clark lifted the receiver, listened, spoke briefly, replaced it. He stared down at the large-scale map of the division's area, open on the desk. 'That's the Incident van reporting Skagton Wood searched and empty and the lads are moving into Arrow Wood . . . Have you any solid news?'

'I've checked out Hyde and Thurston, sir, and they're both clear.'

'Who else is on the list?'

Normally, Clark would not have had to ask: he had an astonishing memory for detail. 'Drew and Harman.'

'You should have questioned them before returning.'

'I had to pass by here to reach either of them and thought it best to make a report before continuing.'

'Have someone else question them. The first reports from the public of sightings of Elaine are coming in and I want you to check if any of them carry weight.'

'Wouldn't it be better to leave that for the moment . . .'

'You have forgotten the routine for missing persons?'

'But we can be certain Elaine hasn't run away, she was kidnapped in Pearce Wood. So it's certain she won't be out on the roads—'

'Nothing is certain until it's proved. We have reason to believe she was attacked in the woods, but not hard proof. Therefore, all possibilities still have to be considered. Further, I am not having my orders questioned. Is that clear?'

'Yes, sir.'

Perry drove home.

'Is there any news?' Elizabeth asked.

'Nothing,' he answered bitterly.

'But she's got to be found.'

He spoke sharply. 'You think we don't know that,

that we're not doing everything that damn well can be done?'

She gripped his hand. 'I wasn't trying to suggest you weren't. It's just that . . .' She stopped.

'The cavalry ought to have arrived by now. That mostly only happens on the screen.'

'Couldn't she have just wandered off somewhere?'

'And thrown away her mobile?'

'You're sure a man has her.'

'As sure as anyone can be at the moment.'

'Then . . . then she's in the hands of a paedophile and if she's not found very soon, she'll be lucky to be dead.'

She turned away, but not before he had seen her lips begin to quiver.

He ate a fourth piece of toast, drank a third cup of coffee, leaned back in the kitchen chair and closed his eyes. It was received doctrine that no one could commit a crime without leaving traces. But those traces had to be found and their significance understood. When there was a burglary, a mugging, an assault, the crime was completed and the police had the time in which to find the traces and determine what they meant. Here, the crime was not completed, the need was to save Elaine and there was precious, if any, time.

The DI insisted he investigate the reported sightings of Elaine to evaluate whether any were genuine. But if one accepted, despite the lack of hard evidence, that she had been kidnapped, not one of them could be true. So to question those who had reported seeing Elaine had to be a complete waste of time. But in theory, Clark was correct to instruct him to carry out these inquiries. To ignore a superior's command was at best stupid, at worst disastrous. Yet there were occasions when the possibility of disaster had to be accepted.

'You're looking all in,' Sandra said, as she entered the kitchen through the front door on her return from taking Moira to school.

'Which is how I feel mentally.'

'Then upstairs and a nap.'

He shook his head.

'You'll feel much sharper.'

'And miss the chance of calling up the cavalry?' He maybe couldn't blow a trumpet, but he could carry out a far more promising investigation than Clark demanded.

On the far side of the road and at a wide angle to Pearce Wood were two bungalows, one of Scandinavian, the other of who-knew-what design. He knocked on the door of the first, introduced himself to an elderly widow. He was asked into a sitting room, notable for the quality of the painting on the wall and of the mahogany bureau bookcase, its shelves filled with leather-bound books.

Mrs Tobin, in her early eighties, white haired, dressed neatly in unfashionable clothes, her manner that of a woman used to getting her own way, said, 'I cannot think why her mother allowed her to walk through the woods on her own.'

'Mrs Oakley had expressly forbidden it,' Perry said, speaking from the depths of a comfortable chair. 'Sadly, Elaine disobeyed her mother.'

She sighed. 'So much has changed. When I was young, we lived near woods and my sister and I were free to wander through them on our own. You said you'd like to speak to my husband as well as me? I'm afraid he's driven into Carnford and won't be back for a while; but I fear he will be of no help since he was not at home when the poor girl disappeared. And unfortunately, neither will I.'

'Perhaps not directly, Mrs Tobin, but you may have seen or heard something that seems to be of no significance to you, but maybe is to us. So if you'd be kind enough to tell me about yesterday and whether you've recently seen anyone hanging around here or if a car has been parked by the wood . . .?'

She spoke, her voice sharp but pleasant. After lunch she had had a little nap – one of the privileges of age – and then had been in the kitchen where she had cooked curried chicken for the next day's lunch. Curry always improved with waiting. Her husband, having lived in Maharashtra, was very fond of genuine curry – that was, not how some English thought curry should be: hot enough to bring tears to the eyes. Afterwards, she had settled in the sitting room. The road was not visible from the house so she couldn't have seen anyone on it. She was not aware of any car which recently had been parked outside the woods on more than one occasion or of any loitering stranger.

'I'm very sorry, Constable, but as I said at the beginning, I can be of no help.'

Perry thanked her, left. He was halfway to the gate in the well-clipped hedge beyond the bowling-green lawn, when a call stopped him. He walked back to the front door.

'I've suddenly remembered Bill,' Mrs Tobin said. 'So silly of me to have forgotten him. But the older one becomes, the less one can rely on one's memory.'

'He may be able to help?'

'He mows the lawn, keeps the garden weeded – except for the herbaceous border, since he will drag up plants without making certain they are weeds, so I do that. He was here Wednesday afternoon, mowing the lawn and so on. I don't know if he might be able to help you more than we can.'

'What is his full name?'

'Bill Young. I don't think there's been a day when I haven't asked him how he is and he's replied, "Getting older, but still young."'

Perry smiled. 'D'you know where he lives?'

'In one of the houses up in the village, but I'm not certain which one. My husband knows, so he can ring you when he gets home.'

'It'll be easy enough for me to find out. Thanks for all your help.'

He returned to the road, walked along to the second bungalow. Here were no carefully mown lawn and weeded flowerbeds full of colour, but all the signs of neglect. He was unsurprised when Louise – as she introduced herself – so obviously gave all her attention to herself. Blonde hair was carefully styled, make-up was generous, clothes looked expensive.

'A real live detective! I don't think I've ever met one before.'

Perhaps he was being ungenerous and she had not once walked the streets. 'You'll know Elaine Oakley is missing; I'm talking to everyone who might be able to tell me something which would help find her.'

'Can't say I know Mrs Oakley, but I've seen the girl often enough on her horse. Poor little kid.'

'May I have a word?'

'Come right in, as the actress said to the hesitating bishop.'

The sitting room was full of colour, but little harmony. Above the fireplace was a large, framed painting of a languorous blue nude.

'What'll you have to drink?' she asked.

'Nothing, thanks.'

'Because you're on duty? What else aren't you allowed to do?'

'Were you here yesterday afternoon?'

'I was with Dotty. Guess what we were doing.'

'Too many options.'

'We were celebrating her divorce.'

'Where?'

'In town. I guess we kind of overdid things since we met a couple of good-looking lads and agreed to go to the Friendly Islands with them. Had a job to persuade them we weren't in that much of a hurry to be friendly.'

'Have you noticed any strange men hanging around the area recently?'

'I should be so lucky!'

He left after she expressed her sorrow at not being able to do more for him.

Eight

The Fox and Hounds was on the highest part of Rickton and enjoyed a view to the south across a wide swathe of the countryside; when the air was very clear, one could see the thin line of the sea.

Pubs could be a good source of information, so Perry drew into the small car park, walked past two other vehicles, and went into the bar, which had avoided gentrification and still offered a traditional setting.

He seldom drank when on duty – not so much because of regulations, but because he liked to keep a clear mind when working – but it would be absurd to stand at the bar with empty hands. He ordered a half pint – no damned litres here, a notice said – of the local real ale.

As Perry was handed a half-pint tankard, he asked the bartender, 'Do you know where Bill Young lives?'

'Turn right out of here, start on down the hill and it's the second cottage on the right. But you'll likely see him in here in a moment; usually turns up for his regular before he eats.'

Ten minutes later, a man entered to whom the bartender spoke and then indicated Perry.

Perry moved along the bar. 'Are you Bill Young?'

'That's me.'

'Can I buy you a drink?'

Young looked at him and, with country directness, said, 'Why d'you want to do that?'

'DC Perry, local CID.'

Young looked surprised. A man further down the bar drank quickly and left. The bartender, taking acceptance of the offer for granted, poured another tankard of ale.

Perry led the way across to one of the tables.

'Something wrong, then?' Young asked as he sat.

'I'm having a word with anyone who might be able to help us find Elaine Oakley.'

'Then I'll do what I can, but it likely won't be nothing.'

'I've spoken to Mrs Tobin and she told me that from her house, she couldn't see the road which runs past Pearce Wood. I'm wondering if you could from the garden?'

'Comes in view when you're level with the main flowerbed.'

'Yesterday afternoon did you see Elaine being dropped by the field in which there's usually a horse?'

'Matter of fact, I was doing the far end of the lawn so yes, I did see Stan drop her. '

'Can you say how long she waited by the field?'

'No. The next minute, the bloody mower packed up and I couldn't get it started again. Keep telling Mrs Tobin they need a new one, only the old boy don't like spending, even though he can't need to worry where the next quid's coming from. So I had to take the mower up to Dick in the village for mending.'

'When you drove back, was Elaine still waiting by the horse field?'

'She'd gone.'

'Then the last you saw of her or Burrell was when he dropped her there?'

'In a manner of speaking.'

'I'm not certain what you mean?'

'Well, like, I didn't see him again, only his van.'

'In the farmyard?'

'By the woods.'

'Which ones?'

'Pearce Wood,' he answered, making it clear he thought Perry was slow-thinking for a detective.

'The van was parked on the road?'

'In The Cut.'

'What's that?'

'Name we use for the short cut at the side of the woods what goes through to Felding Road. Not used much now with being too overgrown and no one walking anywhere.'

'You saw his van there after he had dropped Elaine?'

'That's right.'

'How long was this after he dropped Elaine?'

'Quarter of an hour, maybe. I wasn't long with Dick, him being too busy to do the job immediately or have a bit of a chat.'

'How do you know it was Burrell's van?'

'Seen it often enough.'

'You recognized the number plate?'

'Didn't look at it.'

'Then how can you be certain it was his van?'

'You don't mind asking the same thing time and again, do you? There ain't another white Transit van on the road that's in such a state. Like his farm. There's some calls that a pigsty, only pigs keep their sties a sight better than he does.'

Perry stepped through the open doorway into the detective inspector's room. Clark looked up. 'You are about to tell me you've learned s.f.a. from any of the eyewitnesses?'

'Not exactly, sir.'

'One of the reports could be genuine?'

'I haven't managed to check up on any of them yet, sir,' Perry said carefully.

Clark's anger was immediate. 'Then what the hell have you been doing?'

'I thought it would be useful first to have a word with people in properties on the other side of the road to Pearce Wood and try to gain confirmation that Burrell did drop Elaine by the horse field.'

'You have taken command of the case?'

'No, sir.'

'Merely ignored my orders?'

'Not ignored them, sir – delayed them for a short while.'

'I like smart-talking constables as much as a dose of arsenic and if you reckon you are—'

'Hang on.'

'Godamnit, you've forgotten who you're talking to!'

'I had a word with Young, who does odd job gardening, and he saw Elaine dropped by Burrell at the horse field. Almost immediately afterwards, he had to take a mowing machine up to the village for repairs and on the way back, he noticed Burrell's van was parked in an old track running down along the side of Pearce Wood.'

Clark drummed his fingers on the desk. 'Burrell claims he drove straight back to his farm. So we . . .'

'There's a problem.'

'Which is?'

'Young's identification of the van is based on nothing more than that it was a white Transit in as battered a state as Burrell's. He didn't note the registration number and can't quote any identifying feature.'

'It's all guesswork?'

'For now, maybe. But a search of the area could confirm Burrell had been down The Cut.'

'The search would be unlikely to confirm the time he was there.'

'At least it would be something.'

Clark picked up a pencil and fiddled with it.

'Sir, assume it was his van and then this ties him with Elaine's disappearance. We've found no body so there's reason to believe she's still alive and since the best place to hide her must be on his farm, we must search every inch of that now.'

'Is he likely to give us permission to do so?'

'Obviously not, if guilty; if innocent, probably not because he's a bloody-minded individual.'

'There's no question of a search without a warrant.'

'Now there is the evidence to get one.'

'The facts, as opposed to your assumptions, would not persuade a magistrate.'

'We can't just sit here. We have to find a way of carrying out a search. A child's life is at stake. If we can't get a warrant, we have to go ahead without one.'

'No matter what the circumstances, the law will be observed.'

'Even if it becomes a death warrant?'

'You will carry out my orders and start talking to potential eyewitnesses.'

Like hell, Perry thought.

In sunshine, Morning Farm – house and outbuildings in need of repair, rubbish everywhere, equipment left to disintegrate, poorly-looking animals – was an even more depressing sight than at night. Only the two Dutch barns – the one filled with hay, the other being loaded with sheaves of wheat by Burrell – marked successful farming.

Perry, greeted by the snarling barks of the Rottweiler, walked to the nearer barn and looked up at Burrell, who was standing on the sheaves and was six feet above him. 'You don't often see this old method of harvesting these days.'

'You want something?'

'A chat.'

'Ain't time. After this load's in, there's another in the field to carry.'

'Sounds as if you could do with some help.'

'Not from the likes of you.'

'I worked on a farm when I was young.'

'What was it farming? Mice?'

Perry climbed the small ladder at the side of the wagon and stepped on to the remaining sheaves of wheat. A pitchfork had been stuck into one of them and he pulled it free, speared a sheaf, swung the pitchfork to drop this on those in the barn. 'Looks a good crop.'

'Think I'd grow a bad one?'

He would have considered that likely. 'The stalks look much longer than is usual these days.'

'Because I grow 'em longer.'

He passed another sheaf across. 'Does that makes for better litter?'

'If you ever was on a farm, you didn't learn nothing on it. I grow it long so it sells for thatching to them what can't afford reeds . . . If you're going to clear the wagon before it's tomorrow, stop yammering.'

Perry quickly rediscovered muscles in arms, shoulders, and back and was grateful when he forked across the last sheaf to empty the wagon except for the tailings. Back on the ground, he removed the bits of husk and grain which had fallen on his head and between chest and shirt.

'Don't reckon to waste money hiring you,' Burrell said, as he climbed down. He thrust the two prongs of the pitchfork into the ground.

'Then I'll stick to my present job. In which case, shall we go inside to have the chat?'

Burrell hawked loudly, spat forcefully, walked with plodding steps to the house. Perry followed.

A middle-aged woman was hoovering the carpet in the sitting room. 'You coming in here, then?' she asked.

Burrell grunted an answer.

She switched off the machine.

'Sorry to disturb your work,' Perry said.

'Ain't nothing to be sorry about,' she answered cheerfully. She unplugged the cable, let it run back into the machine, picked that up and left.

'I need to check on what you were doing Wednesday afternoon,' Perry said.

'Why?' Burrell answered.

'Because the boss told me to. So I'd be grateful if you'd talk.'

'And I'd be a bloody sight more grateful if you'd clear off and leave me alone.'

'The moment we find Elaine, no one will bother you and you'll be left in complete peace. And maybe me asking questions is annoying, but you'll want to do all you can to help us find her, won't you?'

'I ain't seen her since I dropped her at the field.'

'Having forgotten to tell her the horse was not there.'

'Weren't no reason to remember.'

'Knowing how fond of the horse she is, it seems odd you didn't mention it wasn't there. Where did you move it to?'

'I told you.'

'Tell me again.'

'To fresh grazing.'

'Wouldn't she have been interested to hear that from you?'

'You think I'd nothing better to do than worry about what she wanted?'

'Perhaps you were more concerned with what you wanted?'

'What you suggesting?'

'Supply your own answer. You dropped Elaine by the field even though she hadn't been able to phone her mother to meet her.'

'How was I to know?'

'Of course. All your attention was on driving . . . She's an attractive kid, wouldn't you agree?'

'Ain't noticed.'

'Auburn hair, deep blue eyes, round, laughing face. There's some men would get excited by her. Are you?'

'What you getting at now?'

'Just curious. You dropped her by the horse field instead of driving her home. What did you do next?'

'Repaired the harvester.'

'You told Mrs Oakley you collected a late cut of hay. Something seems to be confusing you.'

'You are, with all your sodding questions.'

'Then I'll keep them as simple as possible. You didn't collect hay?'

'After I done the repairs.'

'That was a long job?'

'Long enough.'

'What did you do when it was finished?'

'I said. Carried the hay.'

'And that took how long?'

'You think I work to a watch? What's it all bleeding matter?'

'You can't guess?'

'Ain't trying.'

'I need to know what you did after dropping Elaine off.'

'How often do I have to tell you?'

'No need to do so again since you're lying. Soon after you dropped Elaine by the field, you were in Pearce Wood.'

'That I weren't!' he said violently.

'Your van was in The Cut and you were in the woods. What were you doing in them? Chasing a young girl, grabbing hold of her, carrying her away to rape her?'

'I weren't in the wood chasing the kid. I don't know what happened to her and you can bugger off before I throw you out!' he shouted.

The door opened and the woman who had earlier been cleaning the room looked in, her expression showing alarm. 'Everything all right, then?' she asked nervously.

'Fine,' Perry assured her.

She hesitated, spoke to Burrell. 'I'm ready to go back home.'

It was a chance to be seized. Perry stood. 'I was about to leave, so I can drop you home on my way.'

She looked at him, at Burrell, back at him again. 'That would be kind.'

They left the house and crossed to his car to the accompaniment of snarling barks. He started the engine, backed and turned. 'We'd best introduce ourselves and I'd best find out where we're going! I'm Ron Perry, local CID.'

'Maggie Plat. My place is in Rustden, at the back of the church . . . You're trying to find that poor kid?'

'Me and everyone else in the force.'

'And you think he might know?' A jerk of the head indicated the retreating farmhouse.

He drew out on to the road. 'We're asking anyone and everyone if they know something . . . Strange, but you seem to think he might be able to help us.'

'Wouldn't be here if you didn't think the same, would you?'

He smiled. 'You've a point! But to be frank, it seemed to me you'd a reason for speaking?'

'Only . . .'

He was about to prompt her to complete what she had been about to say when she resumed.

'Don't like sounding bitchy . . .'

'No fear of that. Best tell me what's on your mind since it may help. Maybe he's been saying something about Elaine which is worrying you?'

'No . . . not exactly . . .'

'But you're not happy?'

'I didn't realize it until afterwards . . .'

'After what?'

'The child went missing.'

'What did you miss?'

'How he'd changed.'

'In what way?'

'You wouldn't think it, not after him shouting at you like that, but just recent he's been almost cheerful instead of sour as an apple in April. More like he used to be when he kept the farm proper. Used to grow better crops than most and looked after the cows so good they won prizes in the local shows. Yet look at the place now.'

'Did something cause him to change?'

'She did.'

'Who's that?'

'Valerie. Real friendly and always cheerful. There was some said she'd too much of a temper, but as I told 'em, she's a redhead, so what d'you expect?'

'She was his wife?'

'Hadn't got that far, but most thought it would from the way they was together so much.'

'What broke up the relationship?'

'No one ever knew, even if there was plenty said they did. It was sudden. I arrived to do the house and cook and he shouted at me that I was late and he wasn't going to pay for time I wasn't there. Then when she didn't turn up for lunch, like she was expected, I thought she must be ill and asked him what was the trouble with her. That got him shouting like he was going crazy. Learned later Valerie had upped and gone . . . Women can make a man turn odd.'

'And mostly do.'

'You sound like my Will. Says women cause more trouble than a late night at the pub.'

He dutifully chuckled. 'Have you any idea where Valerie is now?'

'Never heard. There's some say she married a man in the City with more money than most of us will ever see. Good luck to her if that's true.'

'He's not been with anyone since?'

'Who'd have him like he's living now?'

'They say love is blind.'

'According to my Will, it has to be when you look at some of the couples what get married.'

'You were saying he's changed.'

'It's not just letting the place become like a junkyard, it's him. Makes me wonder if it's because of her leaving . . . I suppose that sounds daft?'

'Far from it.'

'There's the things he does.'

'Such as?'

'Buying food he can't want.'

'How's that?'

'The baker delivered late yesterday and I was in the house. He gave me three loaves. I said we only ever had one when he delivered and didn't he know that by now? Told me Mr Burrell had ordered three large loaves every time he called. Couldn't understand it. Mr Burrell hadn't been eating all the single loaf before the next one arrived and what was left got thrown to the chickens. So now what's going to happen? Is he buying just to feed the chickens?'

'That does seem a little odd.' Perry's interest flickered.

'It's not all. There's the tins and tins of food. Baked beans, soups, meatballs, spaghetti. Never gone for that kind of thing before. And there's the frozen food he has me buy. If he's eating everything, he'll grow a belly so big he'll only see his feet in a mirror.'

'Quite a thought!'

'And that's forgetting the chocolate. Bars and bars of it.'

'He has a very sweet tooth?'

'It's never been in the house before. Always said it gives him migraine. So why does he buy it?'

'A difficult question . . . When did he start eating like it was for two?'

'Not all that long ago.'

'About the time he cheered up?'

'You know something,' she said thoughtfully, 'it must have been . . .'

'And was that soon after he bought the dog?'

'Likely. That beast'll savage someone one day, mark my words. And if he ever starts letting it off the chain, I'm not working there any more . . .' She stopped, pointed. 'My house is that one over there.'

He drew up outside a semidetached cottage in the shadow of the parish church, notable for having its steeple erected on the ground.

'Kind of you to bring me back,' she said.

'It's been a pleasure,' he answered honestly.

Nine

Perry parked his car, entered divisional HQ, took the lift – working for once – up to the fourth floor, went along to the DI's room; it was empty, as was Yates's. Only Stone was in the CID general room.

'Where's everyone?'

'Ted's dealing with a job, Jock's doing something else.'

'What?'

'Didn't say.'

'Very informative! And where's the brass?'

'Took off as a team.'

'For where?'

'The sarge did look in, but I can't remember . . . Yes, I can.' Stone seemed surprised at this. 'Pearce Wood.'

Stone so often seemed indifferent to what was going on when it did not immediately concern him. Perry briefly wondered if he had shown more interest when a cadet. Perhaps not. When possible, senior DCs unloaded on the cadet all the boring, repetitive, uninteresting work. This dulled initiative, sometimes for good. 'I'll take after them.'

'The super at HQ was on the blower wanting to talk to someone.'

'He talked to you.'

'Someone who could answer his questions.'

'You didn't try to accommodate him?'

'He shut the line down when I said I was the only one here.'

Perry returned to his car and drove off. Despite, or because of, the recent alterations to improve vehicle flow, the traffic in central Carnford was all but gridlocked and it was fifteen minutes before he passed the large, ugly building – very suitable for the bureaucracy it housed – which marked the town's southern limits and the beginning of the countryside. Now, thorn hedges separated fields in patterns that seemed irrational, yet had originally made perfect sense; grass was still green, despite the recent lack of rain; late hay was being baled in large round bales; early corn was being harvested with massive combines; cattle fed in strip grazing, sheep in paddocks; a cock pheasant suddenly speared out of a hedge just ahead of his car and flew away, voiding as it went.

Two cars were parked beyond the ride in Pearce Wood and he drew up behind a Ford Escort. He walked down The Cut, not as overgrown as Young's description had suggested.

Clark, Yates, one constable in uniform, one in forensic garb, formed a small group twenty yards in. As he came up to them, Perry asked, 'What's the picture, sir?'

Clark spoke curtly. 'The undergrowth has been disturbed recently.'

'So he *was* down here!'

'A vehicle was,' Clark corrected.

'Any tyre prints?'

'The ground's too hard to read anything.'

'Any sign of where he went into the wood?'

Clark ignored the question. Yates said, 'There's a branch been broken off there.' He pointed to a ten-foot oak sapling. 'Only nothing to say who and when. It's a negative.'

'You've forgotten you found your oats, Sarge,' the uniform PC said.

'That's enough of that,' Yates snapped. 'Back to the cars.'

'There was a woman down here?' Perry asked the PC.

'Would the skipper be looking so miserable if there had been?' The PC had failed to note Yates had slowed and was within earshot. 'Stopped the line and, all excited, called out he'd found something. Turned out to be a stalk of oats.'

Yates stopped and turned around. 'The colour was different and I couldn't see what it was until I'd parted the nettles.' He spoke defensively. 'You heard the guv'nor, so get back up top, double sharp.'

As the others continued up, Perry walked down to the large patch of nettles which had been indicated. Yates had not been as stupid as the PC had tried to make out. The yellowish stalk provided a sharp contrast to the green of the nettles and at first and distant sight could suggest that here was something which might be important. Wheat, not oats, he noted, and an unusually long stalk . . . He turned and hurried up to the road.

Clark was about to step into the Ford. 'Sir!' he called out.

Clark straightened up, left the door open.

Breathing more heavily than he should – Sandra kept suggesting he ate less – he came to a stop, said, 'Earlier on, I decided to have another word with Burrell and then I drove his daily home.'

'I see.' Clark sounded as if he were chewing ice.

'She passed on some interesting information.'

'Which is?'

'Until recently, he'd been as surly as an un-tipped waiter, then suddenly he cheered up. That was about when Elaine disappeared. He's also been suddenly ordering a lot more grub than usual, including chocolate, which he never eats because it gives him migraine. All that can only mean one thing: he's got Elaine at his place and is feeding her.'

'When did this start?'

'She didn't give a date, but he wanted extra bread on Monday.'

'Elaine didn't disappear until Wednesday.'

'If he didn't kidnap her on the spur of the moment, but had been planning to do so, that makes sense, doesn't it? And there's more.'

'What?'

'The stalk of corn the skipper found was wheat, not oats.'

'Why is that of any importance?'

'Most wheat grown these days is short-stemmed with heavy ears, because that gives a good crop which is easily harvested with a combine. This stalk was long and the ear light. Nowadays a farmer would only grow wheat of that variety for one reason, since by most standards it would be unprofitable: the large stalks are used for thatching when Norfolk reeds would be too expensive. There won't be another farmer within miles who grows it.'

'You know that for fact?'

'No, sir, but one can take it as read.'

'One does not read without words.'

'In this case—'

'Report to me as soon as you return to the station. Is that quite clear?' Clark climbed into the car, slammed the door shut, drove off.

'Wouldn't accept a fire is hot until he put his hand in it,' Perry said angrily.

'There's some who don't believe in flying saucers,' Yates remarked.

Perry had been left to stand in front of the desk in the detective inspector's room; like an errant schoolboy, he thought resentfully. Except that in an age of pinko discipline, to treat a schoolboy in such a manner would probably be branded mental cruelty.

'Did I order you to cease any other inquiries and restrict yourself to questioning witnesses who claim to have seen Elaine?' Clark demanded with controlled anger.

'Yes, sir.'

'Yet you have not done so?'

'Sir, I thought—'

'You disobeyed my orders a second time?'

'My opinion—'

'—is of no consequence.'

'I'm certain Burrell kidnapped Elaine. Unless we find out where he's holding her, she will suffer hell before he kills her.'

'I am in charge of this investigation and I decide how it is to be carried out, not one of my constables.'

'I'm not trying to suggest otherwise, sir, but as I told you earlier, by questioning Burrell again, I learned something from the daily that has to be important and I would not have done this had I been questioning eyewitnesses – his manner changed abruptly from sour to pleasant; he suddenly has far more food in the house than usual; he buys masses of chocolate even though it makes him ill.'

'The reason for a man's choice of lifestyle is his own and can be totally misinterpreted by someone else. It has not occurred to you that there may be other explanations for the extra food other than that it is to feed a captive?'

'No.'

'Then you are making the elementary mistake of determining the consequences of events rather than allowing the events to determine the consequence. There are always those ready to believe the world is about to be overcome by catastrophe and who take steps to try to survive. Burrell might well be one such.'

'If he were that kind of crank, Mrs Plat would have mentioned it. And why would he buy chocolate for himself?'

'It is highly nutritious. He might well regard a migraine as preferable to starvation.'

'If it was not his van in The Cut, how did that stalk of wheat get in the nettles?'

'You have proof no other farm in the area grows that kind?'

'I haven't yet had time to make inquiries locally. If the grower is not local, it's very unlikely he would be in The Cut.'

'You have sent the stalk to Forensic to see if they can match it with a stalk from Burrell's farm?'

'No, sir.'

'Why not?'

'Because it would take God knows how long to get a result and we haven't time. We must find Elaine now, not next month, and that means when necessary acting on probabilities. Ignoring Young, Burrell was the last person to see Elaine. He left her by the horse field. He did not take her home because, he told her mother, he had to carry hay; yet he told me he had had to repair his harvester. Before picking up Elaine, he claimed to have visited the scrapyard in town and bought the spare part he needed; Young George said he did not. He hurried to deny he'd ever touch Elaine when I'd made no such suggestion. He bought a guard dog shortly before Elaine disappeared and now no one can get near the place without its warning him. His van was seen in The Cut soon after she disappeared. The stalk of wheat proves he's been there recently. Pointers on their own, I know, but put them together and they're as good as proof.'

'They are not, unless one has a preconceived conclusion. To make two different statements about what one did in the past can be from careless thoughtlessness; the owner of the scrapyard is more likely to be honestly mistaken than Burrell because of the number of customers on any one day; in a time when the activity of paedophiles is all too often news, it is hardly a sign of guilt when a man who has been in a situation in which he might be accused of impropriety hurries to deny that. Burrell told you he bought the dog as a deterrent against theft and the fact he did so not long before the girl disappeared may well be pure coincidence. There has been no established identification of the van seen in The Cut, only a presumption because of the similarity in make, colour, and condition; unless it is proved the stalk of wheat came from Burrell's farm, it is proof of nothing.'

'With respect, sir, you're judging each fact on its own without reference to anything else.'

'I am judging them as they require to be judged.'

'There isn't the time to work to the book.'

'No case can warrant not doing so.' Clark leaned back in his chair. 'Very recently, when talking to Sergeant Yates, I remarked that it seemed to me you were not working with the necessary emotional detachment required in a case such as this. He told me he had come to the same conclusion and so had asked if you were in any way connected to the victim; you emphatically denied this. However, he has very recently spoken to someone who casually passed the remark that it must be a really tough case for you because of the relationship. Are you related to the victim?'

It was useless to continue to deny this. An official inquiry would very quickly reveal the truth. 'Mrs Oakley is my sister.'

'You will be aware of the regulation forbidding an officer to work in a case in which a close relative is involved unless given permission by a senior officer to do so.'

'Yes, sir, but—'

'And you understand the necessity for this rule being observed because if it is not, at trial the defence can challenge and invalidate an officer's evidence on the grounds of partiality?'

'Yes, sir.'

'It is deeply regrettable that an officer in my command should act with such blatant disregard for the rules. You leave me no option but to forward a report on the matter to the superintendent. In the meantime, I would dismiss you from the case were it not necessary to devote every possible effort to finding the child. Therefore, you will carry out the orders you have chosen to ignore until now and will question those witnesses who claim to have seen Elaine following her disappearance. Since another officer will be detailed to follow up any possibility that the person concerned did indeed see the child, your continued participation in the case will not risk further damage.'

About to speak, Perry checked the words. What he wanted to say had all been said before.

'You will talk to each person on the list and if there is any reason to question them further, you will report the fact to Sergeant Yates. You will not without my permission carry out any inquiries which could directly or indirectly concern Burrell.'

Perry left.

As he was passing Yates's room, he was called in.

'Well?'

'I'm restricted to questioning the possible eyewitnesses on the list.'

'Hardly surprising. You've been a bloody fool.'

'Possibly.'

'For sure. You'll never get rid of the black mark on your record.'

'So what would you do, Sarge, if your niece disappeared and there was every reason to believe she'd been grabbed by a paedophile you could name? Sit back and hope?'

Yates spoke slowly. 'Perhaps I might have found the guts to do what you did.'

'Then why pass on to the guv'nor what you'd been

told about me probably being emotionally affected by the case?'

'If you want the sordid truth,' he said bitterly, 'there was every chance the guv'nor would hear what I'd been told and if I hadn't passed it on to him, I would have been in the shit. I need a pension when I retire.'

Ten

'Elizabeth phoned again while you were away,' Sandra said, as she returned to the kitchen after greeting him on his return. 'She was practically hysterical.'

'Hardly surprising.' Perry pulled out a chair from under the kitchen table and sat.

'Couldn't go on living if the worst happens. I did what I could to calm her down . . . Elaine will be found, won't she?'

'Everyone is breaking his back to make certain she is. Everyone but the guv'nor, that is. Won't climb out of the rulebook.'

'You're not giving up hope?'

'No. But hope can become a luxury.'

She crossed to where he sat, put her arms around his neck and lightly pressed herself against his head. 'It's not like you to be so gloomy.'

'I've named the bastard. I've uncovered enough evidence to warrant going in now and searching his farm. So what happens? After a lecture on obeying the rules, I'm sent packing.'

'How d'you mean?'

'The guv'nor's thrown me off the main investigation and left me to waste time questioning people who claim to have seen Elaine after her disappearance.'

'Why do you call that a waste of time? If she's been seen, she must be alive and when you find out who she was with . . .'

'She can't have been sighted.'

'How can you be so sure until you've spoken to the eyewitnesses?'

'Elaine was kidnapped in the woods and is being held by Burrell on his farm.'

After a moment, she asked, 'Could it be to make Elizabeth pay a ransom?'

'No. There's been no demand and won't be. He's a paedophile.'

'Then if he's on the sex offenders' list and you say there's enough evidence, surely you can arrest him?'

'He isn't on the list and he's no previous convictions.'

'Then could you be making a terrible mistake?'

'No.'

'How can you be so certain?'

'You're beginning to sound like the DI. What keeps you arguing? The truth is too grim to face?'

She released him, crossed to the stove, opened the oven door, looked inside, closed it. She straightened up. 'What are you going to tell Elizabeth?'

'Not the truth until I have to.'

He drove slowly, checking the numbers of the semi-detached houses on his left. He stopped in front of No. 16.

What had been the small front garden was now pebbles through which ran a crazy-paving path to the front door. Above this was a fanlight, set in stained glass, the pattern of which he was trying to distinguish when the front door opened to the length of a security chain. He addressed the gap between door and jamb. 'Mrs Barratt?'

'Yes?'

'DC Perry, local CID. Here's my card.' He held this up to the crack.

'Why are you here?'

'You reported seeing Elaine Oakley.'

'One moment, please.' The door was shut, he heard the chain's being withdrawn, the door was opened and he faced a middle-aged woman, nearly a foot shorter than he, with a beaky face and dressed in a colourful patterned frock.

'I'm so glad you're here, I've been waiting and hoping,' she said in a rush of words. 'Do come in.'

He stepped inside. 'I'd have been here much sooner if I could. We've been inundated by the work.'

'You haven't found the poor child?'

'Sadly, not yet.'

'It's so terrible. I hate watching the television and seeing her look so cheerful in the photograph they show when now it must be terrible for her, but I so long to hear them say she's been found . . . But I am leaving you just standing here. Do please go on in there.' She pointed.

An anthropomorphic sparrow, he thought, as he stepped into a sitting room which immediately recalled his aunt's home where untidiness had been regarded as one of the mortal sins.

'Do sit down. And would you like something to drink – tea or coffee?'

'Coffee would go down a treat, Mrs Barratt.'

'It's only instant, I'm afraid, because I drink tea.'

'I drink instant at home.' That was a lie. Since Sandra had bought an electric coffee-making machine, she had banned instant.

'I won't be a moment.' She left.

He settled on a comfortable chair, stared at a framed print above the blocked-in fireplace. A windjammer under full sail. He let his mind wander. He'd always wished he'd had the chance to sail on one and hear the shrill of the wind in the rigging, the thrashing of the sails, the rush of escaping sea through the clanging ports . . . Soon after they had got engaged, Sandra had been amused when he'd mentioned his wish. 'You'd enjoy eating weevily biscuits and salt cod? You'd welcome being soaked all day and night when you object to a couple of raindrops down your neck? You'd cheerfully wake up and jump out of the hammock if called on deck to do something to the sails when you are so reluctant to wake up and positively hate getting up . . .' She had blushed as she had finished speaking. Unlike most of her contemporaries, she had been embarrassed by the thought that she slept with him when not married. 'You, my darling, are a hopeless, unrealistic romanticist.'

Mrs Barratt returned with a tray on which were silver coffeepot, milk jug and sugar bowl, cups and saucers and two slices of fruit cake. She hoped he liked fruit cake – she'd made it the day before. She paused, was undecided, finally asked if the police hoped to find Elaine soon. There was, he said, after hastily swallowing a mouthful of fruit cake, always hope. Much easier to believe that if your job did not make you familiar with tragedy and it was not your niece who was missing. 'Will you tell me about the girl you saw whom you believe was Elaine?'

'I should have reported what I saw to the police immediately, I know. I couldn't sleep when I heard the poor girl was missing, kept thinking if maybe I'd spoken at the time . . . But I was . . . well, afraid of making a fool of myself. The child could so easily have been with her father or a close relative and become fractious. Children do and it's so difficult these days to administer any discipline. When I was young . . .'

'I'm sorry, but if you could tell me the details?'

'Of course. On most Wednesdays I have lunch in

Carnford with Jill who's an old friend. We go to the Park Hotel. I'm sure you know it?'

'Yes, I do.'

'They serve nice food and it has such a pleasant atmosphere.'

Some months before, he had been watching the hotel, his brief to judge whether it was being used by prostitutes with the connivance of the manager.

'We always seem to have so much to talk about and it was quite late when we said goodbye and I walked up to the delicatessen to buy some of the mature cheddar they sell. So much more flavour than the cheese you buy in a supermarket. I bought a pound – a real extravagance, but I do like it so – and I was walking back towards the High Street when a car drew up at the lights. A girl got out of the back and walked away very quickly. The man left the car, in spite of everyone behind, caught up with her and said something, she shook her head, but he took hold of her arm and forced her into the car.'

'Did she struggle?'

'Not really.'

'He only held her by one arm?'

'Yes.'

'She didn't try to hit him with the other?'

'I don't think so.'

'Would she have seen you?'

'She must have done.'

'Were there other people around?'

'Quite a few.'

'Did she cry out for help?'

'No.'

'Did he make her get into the front or the back of the car?'

She thought. 'The front.'

'He must have gone round the car to get back behind

the wheel. Did she make any attempt to get out of the car while he was doing that?'

'She didn't move.' She drank, replaced the cup on the saucer, stared directly in front of her. 'When I saw all about her on the television, I was convinced it was she. What can she be suffering because I didn't try to do anything to save her? But I just thought the man was her father or a relative who was trying to get her to do what she should. If only I had realized.'

'Will you describe her and what she was wearing?'

She did so.

'You say her hair was red. How red?'

'The kind that gets a girl called carrot-tops.'

'Straight or curly?'

'Straight.'

'Long or short?'

'Long, in what seems to be the modern fashion – all straggly.'

'You describe her as wearing a dark blue dress. Could you be mistaken about the shade?'

'Certainly not.' The possibility seemed briefly to annoy her. 'It was the colour of the dress I wore on my twenty-first birthday party when my dear papa took us to the theatre in London and afterwards to a meal at the Savoy. Or was it the other way round? I forget . . .'

'Mrs Barratt, thanks to what you've told me, I can say for certain that the girl you saw was most definitely not Elaine Oakley. Most probably she was, as you originally thought, a daughter who was having an argument with her father.'

She paused, then said uneasily, 'You're not saying that to stop me blaming myself?'

'Elaine's dress was light blue; her hair is auburn and it's curly.'

She said breathlessly, 'If you could know how much it

means to me to learn I have nothing to blame myself for! But that's being so selfish, isn't it? If it had been she, I might have been able to help you.'

His questioning, as he had been so certain, had been a waste of time. Yet in another sense, since it had comforted her, it hadn't.

Eleven

Molverton had had the reputation of being one of the most charming small towns in the county; ten years' development had financially benefited a few people and destroyed much of the charm.

It was not somewhere Perry knew well and after ten minutes of searching, he drew up outside a fishmonger and went in to ask for directions. As he waited to speak to an assistant behind the iced counter, he noticed a large Dover sole to the side of three salmon. If Sandra were asked, 'Caviar, foie gras, or smoked salmon?' her answer would be Dover sole. Being someone with too much empathy for others' suffering, she was under considerable emotional distress and an unexpected treat might bring her some relief, however brief. In his pocket were five pounds, intended for his living expenses, but self-sacrifice was said to be character enhancing.

'Yes?' asked the assistant.

'How much is the sole?'

The assistant told him. He whistled his astonishment. Sadly, if Sandra were to have a treat, it would not be Dover sole. 'Not today, I'm afraid.'

'They feed 'em on gold.'

'Diamonds, more like . . . Can you tell me how to find Easterly Road?'

'Turn right from here, then first – no, second left.'

Moments later, he rang the bell to the side of the front

door of a terrace house, then turned to watch an open Bentley trundle up the road, strap over the long, louvred bonnet, aero screens, outside handbrake, and deep, burbling exhaust promising earthquake power. The dream of every true motorist. Years before, he could have bought one such battleship for a few hundred pounds; now they could be worth hundreds of thousands. If one had as much foresight as one had hindsight, one would be a good sight the richer.

The door opened. 'Yes?' said a middle-aged man, beer belly exaggerated by a low, tightly drawn trouser belt.

'Is Mrs Gore at home?'

'What's it to you?'

'I'd like to speak to her. County CID.'

'Here, are you saying she's done something?'

'I merely need to talk to her about the report she made saying she thought she had seen Elaine Oakley.'

'You had me worried she'd been robbing a bank and not shared the loot.' Gore sniggered. 'I suppose you'd best come in.'

The front room was as untidy as Mrs Barratt's had been tidy. Pages of the *Daily Mirror* were on the floor around the settee; two empty cans of lager and a dirty plate with knife and fork were on the mantelpiece; a single slipper was in the middle of the carpet.

Gore went out, returned with his wife. She could politely be described as solid. Her blonde hair was dark at the roots; make-up had been laid on rather than applied, particularly the green eye shadow; a double chin loomed, and her cotton dress was under strain. She looked at Perry, then at the pages of newspaper, the empty cans, the single slipper. She addressed her husband. 'What's up with you, then?'

'How d'you mean, love?'

'Bringing a visitor in here with the room like this? What

will he think? That I spend my time playing bingo down at the old cinema?' She collected up the pages and dextrously fitted them together, placed the two empty cans on the plate, picked that up, demanded her husband find the other slipper and take them up to their bedroom, hurried out.

'Gets upset easy,' Gore muttered as he settled into a chair. 'Always going on and on about things.'

She returned. 'It's him working at nights this month what's the trouble,' she told Perry. 'Always the same. On at nights and he don't care what mess the house is in. Born in a cellar.'

Perry tried to be diplomatic. 'I never find a little untidiness disturbing.'

'It annoys me something rotten.' She took up station in front of the fireplace. 'He says you're here about me seeing the girl?'

'Yes. And if you'd—'

She interrupted him. 'I was in the centre of town in the afternoon and see her come out of the baker's. Eating a bun. A man comes up to her and she didn't want to go with him, but he made her. Didn't think no more of it until the telly news about the missing girl. It was her I saw.' She addressed her husband. 'Didn't I tell you it was?'

'Yes, love. Only like I said—'

'She didn't want to go with him.'

'Did he take hold of her roughly?' Perry asked.

She hesitated. 'I don't know I'd say that . . .'

'Did she try to run away from him?'

'No, not really.'

'But since he wasn't holding on to her very firmly, she could have done?'

'I suppose so.'

'Will you describe her?'

'Why?'

'I have to make certain the girl you saw was Elaine.'

'I've just told you.'

'What colour was her hair?'

'Red.'

'How red?'

'Like on the telly.'

Due to a trick of lighting, Elaine's hair as seen on her photograph on the television had appeared to be red, not auburn. 'Was it short, long, curly, straight?'

'Long, in a ponytail and looked real nice, not like some of 'em these days.'

'Her dress was what colour?'

'Blue.'

'Light, medium, or dark blue?'

'Dark.'

'Then it's many thanks for getting in touch with us, Mrs Gore, but the fact is, the girl you saw was not Elaine Oakley.'

'You calling me a liar?'

'Of course not. And as I said earlier, we're very grateful to anyone who calls us, but Elaine's hair is auburn, not red; she does not wear her hair in a ponytail; her dress was light, not dark blue.'

She spoke angrily. 'You'd do a sight more good looking for her instead of coming here and telling me I didn't see what I see.'

'I quite agree.'

She could not understand his answer.

The house, in the village of Beach Under, less than four miles from Molverton, was on the edge of a playing field, donated years before to the village by an elderly sea captain. On the opposite side of the road was a butcher who, despite the supermarkets in nearby towns, continued to enjoy a strong trade since he offered quality.

The house was old, small and possessed a quirky character thanks to gentle subsidence which had slightly altered the lines of the bricks. There were leaded-windows; a porch with iron-hard, darkened oak uprights; a wide swathe of Virginia creeper which was slowly plucking out the mortar between the bricks; and a garden filled with colour, in one corner of which was a weeping willow, weeping copiously.

He parked on the road, opened the gate, walked up the brick path, entered the porch, knocked on the panelled oak front door. The door was opened. 'Mr Jameson?'

'Yes?'

'Constable Perry, local CID.'

'Come on in.'

In his late seventies, Perry judged. Beginning to shorten with age, but still held himself sharply upright and dressed carefully: blazer with badge on the breast pocket – regimental? Spoke with care, acted with courtesy. A type of man who had become the butt of snide jokes because he represented past times.

The room he stepped into was lightly beamed; the furniture and furnishings suggested foreign lands. A black lacquer cabinet was vaguely similar to one a cousin owned and had reputedly been brought home by an ancestor from Shanghai in the nineteenth century and was very valuable – everything his cousin possessed was claimed to be very valuable. Two small bronze Buddhas, one on either side of the fireplace, beamed their contentment. The brightly coloured, strongly patterned carpet was Indian.

'The lady wife is out,' Jameson said, 'at a bridge party; a nattering party I call 'em. There's no charge for sitting.'

Perry sat. If the heavily carved chair had come from abroad, it had been from somewhere where comfort was not greatly appreciated. 'I'm here because of the report you made.'

'Not found the poor kid yet, then?'

'No.'

'Beastly business. As my lady wife said, the more you learn about human nature, the less you appreciate it. Knew a man a couple of years back who couldn't say boo to a goose. Yet one day he killed his wife with an axe, got into his car and drove to the police station, turned himself in. Seemed she had been bullying him for years and he'd reached the point where he couldn't take any more. The court was lenient after hearing about the life he'd led, but he still received six years. Often wondered how he got on in jail, being a man who liked watching birds and walking his dog which never obeyed any of his orders . . . But you're not here to listen to me rambling on, are you?'

'Still, very interesting,' Perry said diplomatically.

'Now, what can I tell you?'

'First, where you were when you saw this girl.'

'I'll have a cigarette before I start if you don't mind? Do you smoke?'

'No.'

'But you'll join me in a tot?'

'I won't, thanks, because I've a fair bit of driving to do when I leave here.'

Jameson stood. 'Damned laws! Can't have a decent meal out these days, not with all this drinking and driving nonsense. If the shambles of a government had some good red wine with their meals, they wouldn't be the useless bunch of toads they are . . . Won't be a moment.'

He returned to the room with a glass in one hand and a lighted cigarette in the other, sat. 'The lady wife keeps on at me to give up smoking and to drink less, but as I tell her, what other pleasures are left at my age?'

'When and where did you see this girl, Mr Jameson?'

'Sorry, wandered off again. She often says I never keep a conversation on track . . . It wasn't long after the telly said she went missing. I was in Marks and Spencer – like their cheese. I was waiting at the checkout when she came up behind me, pushing a trolley with a bar of dark chocolate in it. Surprised me. Kids usually don't like dark chocolate.'

'You had a reason for noticing her?'

'I thought I'd just explained,' Jameson said huffily. 'Couldn't understand why she'd bothered with a trolley if all she wanted was a bar of chocolate.'

'Will you describe her?'

'Young; between seven and ten, I'd say, but I'm no good at judging. Youngsters look older than they are and women do all they can to look younger. An attractive kid. Curly auburn hair, round face, dark blue eyes, dimpled chin. I'd call her tall for her age, but everyone seems to be growing taller these days. There was a sparkle about her. Know what I mean?'

'I'm afraid I'm not quite certain.'

'Full of fun and a little devilment. When I saw the photo on the television, I thought the face looked familiar and then I remembered the girl at the checkout. Certain they were one and the same.'

The description, especially the reference to the girl's sparkle, forced Perry to accept that this might have been a genuine sighting of Elaine. If that were so, she had not been seized by Burrell and, largely because of his insistence that she had, the thrust of the search had not been to learn where she might have voluntarily gone after leaving the horse field . . .

'She lived in South Africa when she was younger, then?'

'Who?'

'The young girl, of course.'

'What makes you think that?'

'Never mistake a South African accent. Like Australian and New Zealand ones. I wonder if there are some of them who think we have a noticeable accent.'

'The girl you've described spoke with an accent?'

'A yarpie one, only I expect you're not allowed to say that now with all this political correctness nonsense.'

He had not seen Elaine.

There were two more names on the list of potential eyewitnesses, their addresses quite near each other in the west of the county. The journey was cross-country, and with no major road going from east to west, would take time even if the traffic were light. He was tired, having worked since early morning, hungry, and convinced their evidence would prove to be as valueless as all he had heard so far, but the job had to be completed.

Three quarters of an hour later, when the first touch of night had altered the quality of the blue of the sky, he drew up outside a block of flats designed by an architectural philistine, their ugly, utilitarian lines highlighted by the nearby centuries-old church half ringed with a tall yew hedge.

A lift took him up to the fifth floor and a quick walk along to flat 54. He rang the bell to the right of the door; when there was no response, he rang it for longer. Behind him, a door opened and he turned to see a middle-aged woman in the doorway of the flat on the opposite side of the small square.

'If you want the Camerons, they're out,' she said.

'Have you any idea when they'll be back?'

She hesitated to answer and he judged she was doubtful about giving any further information. 'Detective Constable Perry, county CID.' She regarded him with curiosity. 'Do you know if they'll be back soon?'

'They won't be since they left a day ago to fly to their house in Portugal where they spend much of the summer enjoying the sun.'

'Then there's no point in my waiting.'

'Shall I tell them when they come back that you called?'

Clark might demand he phone them in Portugal to question the wife. 'That's kind of you, but I think it'll be more to the point if you'll give me their telephone number.'

'I'm sorry, but I can't do that. You see, they live in the countryside and don't have a telephone so if they want to speak to anyone, they have to use a public one.'

He thanked her for her help, returned to his car, drove through six miles of rolling countryside to Heston Court.

Headlights, recently switched on, picked out opened wrought-iron gates in an intricate design. He turned off the road and drove through the gateway, passing a small square of service houses to continue up a curving gravel drive. Initially, the main house was not visible because of rhododendron bushes and ancient oak trees and he visualized an Elizabethan manor filled with history and suits of armour; reality proved to be a large Edwardian pile in which visual grace played no part.

The portico would not have disgraced the manor he had imagined: the two heavy oak doors were studded; to their right was a wrought-iron bell pull in the shape of a ring in a lion's mouth. He pulled and there was an electric buzz, not a jangle of bells. Tradition retreated further.

The right-hand door was opened by a woman in her early twenties, wearing an apron over a dress, which accentuated the angularity of her figure.

'Is Miss Jill Pike in?' he asked.

'That's me.' She smiled and her features, which had appeared slightly severe, relaxed and suggested a good sense of humour.

He was momentarily nonplussed. The only information he had was the name of the informant and he was talking to her, but was she the daughter of the house, working due to lack of staff, or an employee?

'Are you from the police about me seeing the girl who's missing?'

He introduced himself.

'Come in. Mr and Mrs Achinson are out so we can use the green room.'

He was grateful that unwittingly she had resolved the question. He stepped into the hall, only one floor high and with no hanging tapestries, patterns of weapons on the walls, or suits of armour. He had been in smaller houses with more imposing entrances.

The green room was not predominantly green and was furnished for comfort and watching television. They sat and he asked her to tell him how, when, and where she had seen Elaine. Twenty minutes later, he thanked her, explained that following what she had told him, he could assure her she had not seen Elaine.

'I'm glad of that.' She spoke slowly. 'It's horrible thinking you may have seen a child being abducted.'

'I'm thankful to have been able to ease your mind.' He stood. 'I needn't bother you any longer.'

She said, 'It's a small world.'

And an often disturbing one. He was about to tell her he must hurry away when she continued.

'When I was serving coffee, the news came through on the television and Mrs Valerie Achinson was quite shocked and said she knew the girl. That was why I looked at the screen and saw the photograph.'

His interest was immediate. 'Have you any idea how she could have known Elaine?'

'She just kept saying how it made her feel upset because she'd often seen the missing girl riding. Mr Achinson became rather annoyed.'

'He didn't understand why it should worry her?'

'I suppose it was something like that.'

'Not very sympathetic?'

She spoke hesitantly. 'Different way of looking at things, probably.'

'The rich usually look at everything differently. Well, thanks for your help.'

'Not been much use, have I?'

'On the contrary.'

'When I can't have seen Elaine?'

'Your report could have been vital, so it was of use.'

As they stepped into the hall, they heard car doors slam. Both front doors were swung back and a man and woman entered.

'Good evening, Mrs Achinson, Mr Achinson,' Jill said.

Achinson ignored the greeting. He stared at Perry. 'Who are you?'

Too grand to bother about manners, Perry thought. His wife was considerably younger than he, beautiful and perfectly presented; her red hair had been fashioned by an expert, her make-up was subtle, and even to his ignorant eyes, her dress had cost a small (or large) fortune; the jewels she wore would make any thief's fingers itch. 'Detective Constable Perry, county CID.' By chance he had still been covertly admiring Mrs Achinson and he noticed her apparent, brief dismay.

'Has some bastard broken into the house?' Achinson demanded angrily.

'Happily, nothing so dramatic,' Perry answered. 'I came to have a word with Miss Pike.'

'What's she been up to?' The question was not intended to be a humorous one.

Jill spoke angrily, annoyed by the inference. 'Mr Perry came to speak to me about Elaine.'

'Who?'

'The girl who's missing.'

'Why ask you about her?'

'I thought I'd seen her the day she disappeared and I got in touch with the police. It seems I was wrong.'

'Then that's the end of it.' He spoke to Perry. 'You have nothing more to do here?'

So sod off. Not interested in learning whether any progress had been made in finding Elaine.

Back on the road, Perry judged the Achinsons' relationship to be that old story: money buying youth and beauty. Sadly, youth and beauty was probably now learning the true cost of money. Was she wishing she had married someone of her own age, maybe living in a semidetached and worrying about bills, yet knowing her husband loved her and did not regard her as one more visible token of his wealth?

He passed a field in which was a herd of cows and their eyes glistened in the headlights. It was odd that Valerie Achinson should have become disturbed when he had told her husband his name and rank. Since it was ridiculous to believe her engaged in criminal activity, there must be another reason. The traditional one? An affair with some healthy young buck and she was afraid that he had discovered the fact and would report this to her husband? But that seemed almost as absurd as imagining her to be a thief. She might well be having an affair – and good luck to her – but there surely could be no logical reason for her to think he might learn that fact while trying to find Elaine; and that even if, by some unwelcome twist of fate, he did, he would tell her husband.

He approached lights as they changed to red and braked to a halt. Red for stop; red for danger; red hair for a quick temper. Red hair was not common, yet in this case Elaine and each of the girls mistakenly thought to be she was a redhead. Mrs Achinson was a redhead. More remarkably, she must have lived near Rickton to have often seen Elaine riding . . .

The thought came into his mind that the name Valerie had appeared in the case. When? Why? . . . A mile or so further on, when he had all but given up trying to remember, he identified the name as that of the woman whom many had presumed would marry Burrell. An attractive redhead. Had Valerie Achinson's concern at learning he was a detective been not fear of his exposing an existing affair, but her previous relationship with Burrell? Even the briefest of meetings made him certain Achinson was very conscious of his own image. It would cause amusement if it were known by friends and acquaintances that his wife had once been shacked up with an uncouth farmer who now lived in a property that was little more than a slum.

If this assumption was credible, Valerie Achinson might be able to describe Burrell in sufficient direct or indirect detail to give them an insight into his mind. If her husband were present, Valerie would not answer questions honestly. She must be questioned when he was not at home. Tomorrow was Saturday. Did business tycoons work on Saturdays?

The lights changed to green and a quick blast of a horn alerted him to that fact. He drove forward and the other car roared past him and away, expressing the driver's resentment at sharing the road with the aged and infirm. Parry engaged fourth gear. It was ironic. He had tried to evade wasting his time questioning eyewitnesses who could not have seen Elaine, yet by talking to Jill Pike, he might well have learned something of the greatest importance.

As Perry closed the front door, Sandra, wearing a dressing gown over her nightdress, walked from their bedroom out on to the landing.

'Thank goodness you're back. I was beginning to think you'd have to be out all night. Your meal's in the oven and I'll get it for you.'

'Don't bother to come down. Get back into bed.'

'You think I'm not going to make certain you eat a proper meal?' As she descended, she asked, 'Any luck?'

'The eyewitness reports have proved false, but then that was expected.'

She stepped on to the floor.

'However, there's just a slim chance I might have met someone who can help. The problem is her husband.'

'As it is for every wife.' She kissed him. 'I hope I've managed to prevent the meal drying out.'

'I'm hungry enough to enjoy biltong.'

'I don't think it will be that bad.'

Later, as he ate the stew, boiled potatoes and runner beans, she said, 'Elizabeth was here earlier.'

'Oh. Hysterical?'

'It was always threatening, but never arrived. It's horrible seeing someone suffering such hopeless despair. I did the best I could – coffee and a chat – and in the end she seemed to rally a little. How long has Elaine been missing?'

'Three and a half days.'

'Could she still be alive?'

'In the majority of cases, the girl or woman is raped and left, half alive or dead. No body has been found which leaves the alternative. She's imprisoned and being treated as a sex slave.'

'God! And all because Elaine had a slight row with Liz in the morning and in the evening Elaine couldn't speak to her because the telephone line was blocked.'

'The suffering of a crime so often results from insignificant circumstances.'

'There's a suspect. Why the hell isn't his property being searched from top to bottom?'

'Because the guv'nor demands everything is done by the book and we live in times when the rights of the guilty are more important than the suffering of the innocent.'

Twelve

Perry walked into the CID general room. Gough was sitting at his desk, staring at the VDU with bitter dislike. He looked up. 'Can you make these things work? Tell it to do something and it does something else.'

'They're becoming more and more human.'

Perry went over to the table by the noticeboard, picked up the county telephone directory and carried it back to his desk. He found the number he wanted, dialled.

'The Achinsons' residence,' Jill Pike said.

'Morning, Miss Pike. It's Ron Perry here. Hopefully you'll remember me from yesterday evening?'

'My memory's poor, but not that poor.'

'Are the Achinsons in?'

'Mrs Achinson is, but he isn't.'

'When is he likely to be back?'

'It won't be before late afternoon. He's playing golf and having lunch at the clubhouse.'

'I'll be along in about an hour's time to have a word with Mrs Achinson.'

'I'm afraid she'll be going out before then.'

'Suggest she cancels whatever she was going to do and waits for me to arrive to avoid my having to turn up this evening and disturb her dinner.'

'Frankly, I don't think she'll take any notice.'

'You may well be surprised. See you later on.' He said goodbye, replaced the receiver.

'Now the damn thing's crashed!' Gough said angrily.

'Because you pressed the wrong tit.'

'Tell me something I don't know . . . I forgot to say, the skipper's been around more than once, shouting for you.'

'What's got him hopping?'

'He didn't say, but if I were you, I'd look out for squalls.'

'Is he in his room?'

'He was ten minutes ago.'

Perry hesitated. Yates would want to know what he had learned from the eyewitnesses he had questioned. If he explained why Valerie Achinson should be questioned, he would be shunted to one side and one of the other DCs would be sent to question her. Whoever that might be, he probably would not be so convinced of Burrell's guilt and would not risk questioning her sharply; if smart, she might even persuade him she had hardly known Burrell.

Yates was in his room. As so often, he indulged in schoolboy sarcasm. 'Very kind of you to turn up when you had a spare moment. I hope it hasn't upset your plans?'

'I was hard at it until after midnight, Sarge, so reckoned I was entitled to a little leeway.'

'It's me who decides that.' He picked up a pencil and fiddled with it. 'What did you learn?'

'The witnesses all saw a redhead of about the right age in circumstances which, after they'd seen the news about Elaine's disappearance, made them believe the child had been acting scared. None of them could possibly have been Elaine.'

'That's all?'

He needed time, unaccounted for, to question Valerie Achinson. 'The Camerons were away, but the woman in the next flat said they'd gone to see friends and probably wouldn't be back until late. So I reckon to drive back and question them now.'

'Don't take all day.'

Jill opened the front door and he greeted her. 'Well?' he asked.

'She cancelled her date and is here,' she answered, her tone expressing surprise.

'I'm glad I haven't wasted a journey.'

'Is there some sort of trouble?'

'Not exactly.'

She clearly wanted him to say more, but he merely smiled. He stepped into the disappointing hall.

'She's in the green room.'

Valerie sat in one of the luxurious armchairs, watching horse racing on the large flat-screen.

He greeted her, she ignored him as she watched.

The rank outsider won and the commentator remarked that anyone who had backed it would be drinking champagne.

'I can't think why you're bothering us again,' she finally said, continuing to watch and not bothering to look in his direction. 'Neither my husband nor I know anything about the missing girl.'

'I've no reason to think either of you do.'

'Then why are you here?'

He sat. 'Because you may be able to help us in our search for Elaine.'

'That's ridiculous.'

'Why?'

'You've just admitted we can't know anything about her.'

'You may have some information I'd like to hear.'

'Constable, I have a great deal to do and can't waste any more time, so if you'd please leave.'

'If you insist. But then I will have to return when your husband is here. I doubt you'd welcome that.'

She looked angry and uncertain.

'Before you were married, I understand you lived in or near Rickton?'

'What can it matter where I lived?'

'Did you live there?'

'Yes,' she eventually muttered.

'And you knew Stan Burrell?'

'I can't remember whom I knew or didn't know back then. It's a long time ago.'

'So long that you've forgotten you were going to marry him?'

'Ridiculous nonsense.'

'It's what the neighbours say.'

'Insulting gossip.'

'Gossip often contains a kernel of truth.'

'I wouldn't have married a man like him.'

'Too socially inferior?'

'How dare you be so damned rude!'

'Tell me why you suddenly broke off your relationship with him?'

'There was no relationship.'

'Do I have to explain why I know you're lying?'

Her lips tightened.

'Well?'

'It's nothing to do with you.'

'I wouldn't be here if that were true.'

'How can it matter?'

'Just accept that it does and answer the question. Why did you shrug him off?'

'It wasn't a strong relationship.'

'When the neighbours were certain you'd be married? They have wild imaginations?'

'We were friendly. That's all.'

'But as far as you were concerned, eventually not sufficiently friendly for wedding bells?'

'I . . . I wasn't going to live on scraggy chickens and boiled cabbage.'

'At the time, the prospect was far from that deprived. He was a relatively successful farmer in spite of his lack of capital and machinery. I have heard him referred to as a man with eight green fingers. He owned a house and, since farmers partially live off their own land, enjoyed a reasonable lifestyle. You were working in the village sub-post office and general store for low wages and were living in digs. Since at the time, despite your very attractive appearance, you could have had no reasonable expectation of meeting and marrying wealth, Burrell must have offered at least a reasonable prospect for marriage. Yet abruptly you threw him aside and left the village. I want to know the reason.'

'I won't tell you.'

'I shall have to keep questioning you until you explain.'

She looked away.

He was sorry for her; few wanted their past exposed.

She stood. 'I need a drink.' She crossed to a cocktail cabinet and opened the top leaves, which brought up a shelf on which were glasses and bottles. She poured a whisky. 'Will you . . .?' She stopped.

'Yes?'

'Tell my husband?'

'No.'

She returned to her chair, drank, fidgeted with the glass. 'Do you know why I married Steven?'

'That does not concern me.'

She ignored his answer. 'I met him when I was working as a temporary information guide at a conference. He came up to me and chatted more than once and near the end of the conference asked me out for a meal. He was much older than me, but I was bored. I didn't realize how wealthy he was until we had lunch at the Ritz and the waiters almost fawned around him.

'He asked me out several times and we went to places I'd only ever read about. I came to the obvious conclusion: he was sizing me up as his mistress and this seemed to be confirmed when he kept asking did I know lots of people, go to many parties, had I been to this or that nightclub? I decided he was trying to learn if I'd been enjoying a fast life . . . Do you know what money does to one?'

'I know what lack of it does,' he answered impatiently, uninterested in her post-Burrell life.

'My mother was from a background where to be respectable was to keep one's legs crossed until marriage and not to enjoy uncrossing them afterwards, to have spotlessly clean underwear, and to go to church every Sunday. She had warned me when I was twelve that the men would be around me like bluebottles, desperate to lay their eggs. She knew life. But what she didn't understand, because she never had the chance to learn, was how money distorts everything. Money made Steven not much older than me; it said that in any case an age difference was meaningless; it changed him into a warm and caring man and made virginity ridiculous. So I was ready to become his mistress. But then he proposed to me. I eventually realized why he'd chosen marriage instead of a neat little flat in Chelsea. He needs to possess absolutely and what he possesses must be beyond criticism. He had become satisfied I had not led a wild life, had never been a groupie, would not humiliate him by his friends wondering if I was still a bonus in bed; only if we were married could he make certain I was leading a quiet life.'

'So you didn't tell him about Burrell?'

'You think he'd have had anything more to do with me if he had learned . . .?' She stopped.

'Learned what?'

'Why do you have to know?'

'I've told you. It may help to save Elaine's life.'

'Nothing I say will do that.'

'It's impossible to be certain until you do tell me. What went on between you and Burrell?'

She was silent for so long he thought she still would not answer, but then she suddenly said, 'He was quite sharp when he bothered to be clean and smart; not handsome, but strong. He had the house and made money. There were many locals who would have offered a harder life.' She drained her glass, stood, went back to the cocktail cabinet and poured herself a second drink. Once more in her chair, she said, 'One afternoon I wasn't working and hadn't anything better to do, so I went down to see him. It was hot and he was stripped to the waist, loading hay. Looking at his body moving, seeing the muscles rhythmically flexing, made me feel . . . You know what I mean?'

'I'm afraid not.'

'I . . . I tingled.' She stared directly at him. 'And now I suppose you're going to try to humiliate me more by saying you don't know what that means?'

'I have a reasonable idea.'

'We went into the house and had a couple of drinks. He became as hot as me, so for the first time we moved up to his bedroom and stripped off. The earth didn't move. He wasn't a man. Didn't matter what I did, he was as much use as a broken post rail. I was so . . . so goddamn frustrated, I called him every useless thing I could think of before clearing off.

'He kept pestering me after I told him it was all over. I was resting downstairs in my digs and there was no one else in the house when he turned up. Said we'd try again and he'd prove himself as good as any man. When I refused, he hit me, hard enough to make me dizzy, and started to pull off my clothes. I managed to break free, raced upstairs to my bedroom, slammed the door shut and locked it. He tried to force it open, but couldn't. He became crazy. Some of the things he said he'd do when he got hold of me were sickening. In the end, he went away.'

'Did you report what had happened to the police?'

'It was too embarrassing.'

'You left the village to get away from him?'

'I was terrified that if he got me on my own again, he'd do some of the things he'd threatened.'

Perry again promised no word of what she had told him would ever reach her husband, and left. She had confirmed his darkest fears.

Thirteen

Yates was in his room, standing behind the desk and collecting up papers.

'Sarge—' Perry began.

'If it's not important, I'm off to lunch: didn't have a decent breakfast as I had to get it for myself and the stomach's gurgling like a bath emptying.'

'It couldn't be more important.'

Yates sighed, sat. 'Let's have it. Quickly.'

'Burrell is a sexual pervert . . .'

'Where's the proof?'

'The evidence of a woman he assaulted and threatened with every perversion in the book the moment he got hold of her.'

'Who is she?'

'Valerie Achinson. Before her marriage, she lived in Rickton and was sufficiently friendly with Burrell to consider marrying him.'

'When did you talk to her?'

'This morning.'

'I thought you were interviewing Mrs Cameron?'

'It was infinitely more important to find out what Valerie could tell us rather than question someone who couldn't have seen Elaine.'

'What led you to question her?'

'I was stopped by a red traffic light when I was returning from talking to Jill Pike, who'd reported seeing Elaine, and that made me realize how many redheads had turned up in the case; Mrs Achinson, who employs Jill, is one. And since I'd learned from Jill that Mrs Achinson had lived in Rickton and her first name was Valerie, I wondered if she could be the Valerie—'

'You are back from interviewing this Achinson woman?'

'Yes.'

'You questioned Jill Pike and decided her evidence regarding the sighting of Elaine was of no account, but learned from her certain facts which suggested the wife of the owner of the house might have known Burrell very well and therefore be able to provide evidence of importance?'

'Which she did. I am more certain than ever that Burrell kidnapped Elaine. One objection to his guilt has been that he is not on the sex offenders' list. Now we know—'

'You were ordered by the guv'nor to pass on any evidence you learned which might have a bearing on the case and not to follow it up yourself.'

'What's that matter in the circumstances?'

'The guv'nor will no doubt explain.'

'Obviously, you are under the misapprehension that only you are capable of conducting this investigation,' Clark said angrily.

The angle at which the framed photograph on the detective inspector's desk was set allowed Perry to see the image of his wife. Did she have to live by rules cast in concrete? 'No, sir.'

'Then can you explain why you questioned Mrs Achinson instead of leaving it to someone else to do so?'

'Since no one else was convinced of Burrell's guilt, I decided no one else would pressure her sufficiently to tell the facts.'

'By pressure, you mean threaten?'

'Persuade.'

'I wonder which expression she would use? You have told me she lived in Rickton and was sufficiently friendly with Burrell to go to bed with him, but he proved to be impotent. Later, he wanted to try again. One can hardly be surprised by that.'

'Or that he hit her so hard she was left dizzy?'

'That may well be an exaggeration.'

'Why should it be?'

'She believes she appears in a better light by placing him in a worse one.'

'And she claims he made all the obscene threats for the same reason?'

'Perhaps. Equally, a man can become overexcited when his desires are thwarted, especially by a woman who previously encouraged them.'

'Would the average man respond as he did?'

'There is no such person as the average man on the Clapham omnibus.'

'Can't you understand how, knowing what she's told us, it's even more desperately critical to find Elaine?'

'I understand you are insolently incapable of obeying orders.'

'Sir, when Mrs Achinson jeered at him, told him he wasn't a man, she humiliated him and that made him determined to prove his potency.'

'A dose of Viagra would have done that.'

'He didn't have the chance to find out. She left the area and no one knew where she'd gone so he was deprived of the possibility of erasing his humiliation. Then Elaine came and lived locally. So each time Elaine, whose auburn hair reminded him of Mrs Achinson, was in the van with him, he fantasized using her to recover his manhood. And she could not humiliate him further with her bitter contempt.'

'Are you a psychiatrist?'

'No.'

'Then leave them to talk rubbish.'

'Are you going to search his farm?'

'When there is sufficient proof to apply for, and be granted, a warrant.'

'You can't understand that the moment he satisfies himself, he'll kill her?'

'When we are legally entitled to search his premises, we will.'

Moira wanted to watch a programme on TV which did not start until after her bedtime. She announced she had a pain in her stomach and must rest on the settee until it went away. When that failed to evoke sympathy, she claimed the pain was becoming worse.

'I'll give you some castor oil,' Sandra said.

'What's that?'

'An old-fashioned cure for stomach pains. It tastes really terrible, but never fails to cure the problem.'

'Tastes worse than cabbage?'

'Much, much worse.'

There was a brief silence. 'I think the pain is getting better.'

'Good.'

'I won't need that horrible stuff now, will I?'

'Not if you're fit enough to go to bed.'

Moira left the sitting room and went upstairs.

'The deceptions of motherhood,' Perry said. He stirred the coffee in the cup on the small occasional table.

'You'd rather have her watch that series on TV which you claim is really for morons?'

'You have a point.'

'I'll settle her.'

He watched her go up the stairs and out of sight. How did one make sense of a world in which there were such stark contrasts? Here, at home, was a world of peace and love. Not far away – at Morning Farm to be precise – a young girl was suffering in a way one wished were unimaginable. Did life demand balance? For every honest man, there must be a dishonest one? For one to enjoy a happy life, another must suffer an unhappy one? For a girl to grow up safe, another had to die?

Sandra returned, sat. 'If I knew a friendly genie who'd offer me three wishes, d'you know what they would be?'

'First, to see Elaine safe and sound.'

'Right.'

'Second, a dress from Dior.'

'A terrible waste. That we all go on a holiday to somewhere uncrowded and exotic.'

'And return to bore our friends with photographs?'

'Return with you looking fit and happy. When I was upstairs, Moira asked me if you looked so sad because you'd been drinking castor oil . . . Is there still more trouble?'

'Bitter frustration.'

'You want to tell?'

He recounted what had happened.

'Are you so sure you're right? That this man really is the bastard who has Elaine and will be abusing her so terribly?'

'I can't be sure sure. As Clark told me, I am not a psychiatrist. Even if I were one, I could still be wrong.'

'But you don't think you are?'

'I'm certain I am right . . . Don't tell me that's crazy because one moment I know I'm right, the next I can't be certain.'

'You're terrified he'll kill her?'

'Because he knows I suspect him, sooner or later he'll kill her for his own safety.'

'Is it that impossible to make the inspector understand something has to be done now?'

'How do you teach a statue to talk?'

They were silent until he said, 'You haven't told me your third wish.'

'I'm not going to.'

Perry lay on the bed, staring up at the ceiling, which was hazily visible because street lighting was not entirely held at bay by the curtains. Sandra, on her side facing him, was breathing heavily enough for him to hear the swish of her breath. Her words echoed in his mind. 'Is it that impossible . . .?' The impossible takes a little longer. But the time available was becoming ever shorter. Then how to make Clark understand before it became too late that Elaine was being held by Burrell?

His subconscious must have been working overtime because when he awoke in the morning, he knew what he could do. If he were a fool, that was.

Throughout the day, questions lay between him and what he was doing. When did necessity become foolishness? . . . If the investigation continued along the lines it was on, failure was far more likely than success. Failure meant a child's suffering hell before she died. So, certain Elaine was being held at Morning Farm, how could he not act?

Planning was the key to success. The experiences of those he had arrested had shown him a criminal's greatest threat was an inability to imagine the possibility of failure, to accept nothing could be certain.

Traces were a dangerous threat to any criminal and whilst it might be absurd to consider his intended foray could provoke a full forensic investigation, he had to allow that it might. The clothes he wore – his old and heavily stained overalls, gardening gloves, the plimsolls he had bought when he had almost been persuaded by Sandra to play tennis to help keep himself fit – must be burned and the ashes safely disposed of. He would need something to cover the top of his head because one hair found by Forensics could prove fatal. One of Sandra's hairnets? Did he take a torch? Torches could be inadvertently dropped and left as damning forensic evidence. The moon was nearly full and if the sky was even half clear, no torch should be necessary. He would need meat. There were some lamb chops in the deep-freeze. Defrost one and add four or five sleeping pills – left over from the brief time when Sandra had needed them and found them very efficacious.

How to get to Morning Farm? To leave his car close to there could prove fatal. The sighting of Burrows's van in The Cut showed how one must never assume something would not be noticed; the only safe place to hide it was in full view when it might be noticed, but not remarked. Yet that left the problem of getting from where it was left to the farm. Sandra's folding bicycle.

Fourteen

At night, cars were parked in the road outside the houses in the small council estate – when these had been built, it had not been thought necessary to provide garages. Perry drew up behind a Ford estate and an ancient Vauxhall, satisfied his car would be unremarked, lifted the bike out of the boot, assembled it. He mounted and peddled.

'For men must work, and women must weep . . .' Sandra hadn't been weeping, but fear had made her frightened and tetchy. Wasn't there another way? she had demanded. What if something went wrong? Suppose Burrell believed him to be a thief and shot him?

He reached the foot of the hill and turned left. The sky was clear, the moonlight strong. At the entrance to the yard, he climbed off the bike and laid it down on the verge so that it was concealed by the grass and weeds. He patted his right-hand pocket to make certain the drugged lamb chop was still there, even though it had to be certain it was. Mental tension could make nonsense of certainty. He was reminded of the middle-aged man who, when arrested, had confessed that in spite of the many jobs he'd done, for some of which he had spent time in prison, when he broke into a house, he still felt as if his sphincter would betray him. There was still time to abort the plan; to avoid all risk. Bike back to his car and leave. He met the thought of the relief that must offer by imagining what might be happening to Elaine.

Thanks to the moonlight, he was able to use the bulk

of the two barns to approach very slowly and avoid the slightest sound that might catch the Rottweiler's attention. A vixen called and for a breath-catching instant he mistook that for Elaine's scream; a rustle to his right startled him and caused him to remain still for several minutes: to keep hidden by the barns, he had to concentrate on his route and in consequence not on what lay immediately in front of his feet; he stubbed his foot on a stone and because the plimsoll offered little protection, he almost swore aloud.

He finally reached the nearer barn, paused, then edged his way around it until he could just see the dog. It was standing, head pointing towards him, alert but uncertain. He put his gloved hand in his pocket and brought out the lamb chop. He drew his arm back. At school, the sport at which he had been sharpest was cricket, and at ten yards he had expected to hit the stumps. He called on the gods of cricket to hold his aim steady, threw. His clothing rustled and the dog barked once before the meat landed. It lifted its nose and smelled the air, moved to the right with a rattle of chain, found the chop and ate it.

After a long time, at least as Perry judged it, the dog began to move clumsily then unsteadily settled on the ground. Waiting a further fifteen minutes before leaving the shelter of the barn, he passed the dog, careful to keep beyond the reach of the chain just in case. He settled in the shade of the second barn, nearer to the house.

Burrell was concealing Elaine inside the house or outside. If inside, in a locked room or cellar. Few old houses like Morning Farm had cellars and Maggy Plat cleaned the house during the week and her curiosity would immediately be fuelled by a locked door; further, Elaine, unless secured and gagged, would do everything possible to call for help. An outside prison seemed far more probable. There were the outhouses. She might be in one of those, but their condition was so poor, they could hardly provide security; she might be in some sort of a cage in one of them, but this carried the risk of immediately drawing attention. There were the Dutch barns. Under one of them, a cell-like hole previously dug out of the ground before any crop was stored in expectation of the coming kidnapping. The hay was in two layers, distinguished by colour. The bottom bales were greyish through the weathering of the outside surfaces which meant they were last year's crop; the bales on top were a yellowy brown, which marked them as this year's. Burrell had not known Elaine before Elizabeth and she had moved to their present home, so he would not have built a prison before then. That left the wheat. Harvesting had begun only recently and before then the barn would have been empty. Plenty of time to dig. The sheaves of wheat could be used to conceal the trapdoor yet be easily moved. Which was why he was now going to keep watch until he saw Burrell leave the house with provisions, thereby identifying the underground prison. And if there was no movement this night, because Elaine had been left with enough food and water to last a couple of days, he would return each night until he knew the truth . . .

The front door was opened and torchlight swept across the yard. Burrell stood in the doorway for a while, retreated and closed the door. Perry tried to discern the reason for the other's brief appearance. The dog hadn't barked again and he had made no noise to cause an alarm. So had Burrell merely been confirming all was clear before bringing out the food and water? . . . It gradually became clear this was not so. Disappointed, Perry relaxed. With traffic very light, the sounds of the countryside were clear. It passed the time to identify the hoot of a barn owl, the call of a bulling cow, the croak of a toad, the scream of a rabbit caught by fox, stoat, or weasel.

When the lights downstairs were switched off and those

upstairs were switched on, it seemed he might as well return home, hoping for better success the next night. Or did he accept the absolute need for speed, respond to the demands of emotion, and do what he had promised Sandra he would not, break into the house to learn whether, contrary to his judgment, Elaine was being held inside it? A risk too great? He would be breaking and entering. A policeman sent to jail was a target for every other inmate . . .

He heard the sound of cars travelling at speed on the top road. A local party that had finally broken up? Champagne and caviar or a supermarket's special Chardonnay and ham sandwiches? The cars turned into the lane and headlights swept across the roof of the house, then the outbuildings and barns as they entered the yard.

He only just managed to gain cover on the far side of a barn before being caught in the light. Unable to see, he listened. There were orders. Two men to return to the road and keep their torches working. The others to wait whilst the speaker had a word with Burrell. He recognized the voice. Jenkins, a uniformed sergeant. What blind, shitty luck had brought the police to the farm at that moment? Clearer thought made it obvious Burrell had heard the dog bark earlier, had not ignored this as imagined, had kept watch from inside the house and, thanks to the moonlight and the ruse of appearing to retire to bed, caught sight of Perry and called the police.

He made for a gap in the hedge beyond the yard. Thankfully, Burrell had been too slack to block it efficiently and he was able to ease his way through, at the expense of scratches from the small but vicious thorns. The field sloped up to the first village houses and would have offered him a good escape route had not the moonlight, which earlier he had blessed and now cursed, marked him. Better to stay where he was. Better until the sergeant called out that boy-o was probably hiding on the other side of the hedge beyond the barns.

A man pushed through the gap in the hedge. Perry began to run, tripped over a rabbit hole and crashed to the ground.

'Stand up, chummy, and let's have a butchers at your ugly face.'

He stood.

'Sod me if it isn't Ron!'

Fifteen

'I don't believe it,' Clark said furiously.

Perry stared at nothing. Yates looked even more gloomy than usual.

'I get called out of bed and come here to learn one of my constables, forbidden to have anything more to do with the case, has been caught trespassing on land belonging to the main suspect. Words fail me.' He immediately proved they did not. 'How do we keep the news out of the media? We'll be the laughing stock of the force. Other divisions will still be cracking jokes at our expense this time next year!' He turned to Yates. 'Is the man mad?'

'Impetuous, sir.'

'Ignores every order he's given, argues insolently, pursues his own course irrespective of anyone else. It's a bloody wonder he didn't break into the house and get caught burglarizing it.'

Another few minutes, Perry thought, and he might have given in to wild temptation and been inside. In which case he would now be heading for a charge of breaking and entering.

Clark spoke angrily. 'Suppose you had found the girl? You didn't consider the consequences, did you?'

'Yes, sir. Elaine would have been saved.'

'Don't try to be smart with me. Your trespass would have negated any evidence you gave. You'll never learn, will you? You just charge ahead and to hell with everyone and everything else. You're a one-man disruption. I'm reporting the matter to Superintendent Woolley at county HQ and he will decide what should be done regarding your insane conduct.'

Perry returned to the CID general room.

Gough, on night duty, asked, 'How did it go?'

'The guv'nor's blood pressure went off the scales.'

'And?'

'He's reporting me to the super, so likely in a few days' time I'll be playing the banjo on street corners, hoping someone will drop a coin in the cap at my feet.'

'These days, a banjo won't pluck generous feelings – more likely irritated ones. It's really that serious?'

'You reckon the guv'nor will do anything to ease my fate when he probably claims I've put up such a black against his command that all his chances of further promotion have flown out of the window?'

'It was . . .' Gough stopped.

'Don't bother to tell me it was a bloody fool thing to do.'

'It won't be any consolation, but I reckon what you did shows what policing would be about if the legal eagles weren't all constipated. Frankly, I'd like to imagine I'd have done the same as you.'

Sandra had fallen asleep and only awoke when he arrived home. 'Did you find her?' she asked, as she stood in the doorway of the sitting room.

'No,' Perry answered as he locked the front door.

'I was so desperately hoping you would. Will the nightmare never end?'

'I'm afraid it's going to get worse.' He hung up his mackintosh.

'How?' Her tone had become shrill.

'Burrell called the police to report someone was on his

land trying to steal his junk and since nothing much else was going on, half the night turn arrived.'

'They found you?'

'As any unfortunate man discovers, in flagrante delicto.'

'Surely you explained why you were there?'

'I said I was out for a stroll because I couldn't sleep and lost my way. They seemed reluctant to accept that.'

'For God's sake, don't make weak jokes and be facetious to try and shield me from the truth. I must know what that is. You've got to tell me.' She went back into the sitting room.

He followed her. 'I'd forgotten that Burrell was a cunning bastard.' He described what had happened.

'Surely it's not so terrible to be on his land? People trespass all the time.'

'As I'd told you, Clark had ordered me to have almost nothing more to do with the case. Added to which, if I had found Elaine, my trespass might have badly affected the value of my evidence when charges were brought against him.'

'But if you were looking for her . . .'

'I didn't have a search warrant.'

'Someone had to do something.'

'They'd tell you that everything which can be done is; anything more, can't be.'

'What's going to happen now?'

'Clark's reporting me to the super at county HQ.'

She stared down at her frock, creased from when she had slept on the settee. 'Maybe he'll understand why you did it.'

'Woolley doesn't appreciate failure.'

'You don't think . . .' She became silent.

'I'll be called into his august presence to be told that I'm imitating a bull in a china shop. Make that an ass in a charity shop.'

'What will he do?'

He answered slowly. 'If he listens only to Clark, the odds have to be that I'll be found unsuitable for further service in the CID. I can then either be downgraded to uniform or sent packing.'

'It's that serious?'

'In Clark's eyes.'

'Why does he hate you so?'

'Hate is the wrong word. I disturb him because I undermine his faith.'

'What faith?'

'Subservience to rules, regulations and authority. A man, most especially in the force, should always and unquestionably respect them and whatever the circumstances, obey them to the letter. He finds my attitude not only incomprehensible, but also disturbing because it makes him question himself.'

'Why can't he . . . What's the use? As Uncle John used to say, "We are what we are, not what others would have us be."' She moved forward and put her arms around him. 'Whatever happens, my love, I'm proud you did what you did.'

Clark stepped into the CID general room soon after ten in the morning, looked at the recovered articles which had not yet been taken down to the storeroom; cluttered desks; the reference books which had not yet been returned to the bookcase; the confusion on the table; the disarray on the noticeboard – photographs calling for identification; notices from HQ and the divisional superintendent; notes regarding calls from informers on the special line; a request from a WPC to know who would support a divisional dance . . . 'This place looks like a herd of monkeys has been through it. Clear it up. Perry, interview room one.' He left, slammed the door shut.

'A herd of monkeys?' Stone said.

'Why not?' Fuller asked.

'I thought they came in troops.'

'And break step when they cross a bridge? If the guv'nor says they come in herds, that's how they travel.' Fuller watched Perry move away from his desk. 'Stub a toe, Ron.' For a reason lost in time, though there had to be a connection with the stage's 'break a leg', one did not wish a colleague good luck, but to stub a toe.

Gloomily, Perry reflected that to stub all his toes would not suffice.

The interview room was bleak. The single window was barred; the walls were painted in two shades of institutional brown; the table was scarred; the chairs well worn; the recording machine promised not one incriminating word would be lost; and the framed list of the rights of those interviewed was hardly reassuring.

He moved a chair away from the wall and sat. By the end of the meeting there was every chance he would be out of a job. Woolley was said to damn the slightest mistake. If – when – he was sacked, he would lose his pension and would have to find another job in a hurry. As a security guard? Any prospective employer would want to know why he'd left the force at a relatively early age, and the fact he had been sacked would hardly help. He had risked his future for the sake of family but his family was going to suffer . . .

He had not smoked for some years, but right then he wanted a cigarette. When at school, he had been lucky and escaped any interview with the headmaster for his misdeeds, but now he understood how he would have felt. Ice in the stomach? A bloody glacier.

He stood as the door was thrown open and Woolley hurried into the room. He had a round, almost chubby face with a broad mouth, which could look as if he were about to smile when he had no such intention. He was dressed casually and carelessly, his tie was at half mast, the top button of his shirt was undone and his sports jacket should have been retired. If one ignored the sharp coldness of his gaze and the air of authority, one could mistake him for a good-humoured, well-liked person.

He dropped a battered briefcase on the table, stared at Perry for several seconds, his expression quizzical, said, 'Detective Constable Perry?'

'Yes, sir.'

'Sit.' He settled on the chair behind the table, opened the briefcase and brought out two typewritten pages clipped together. He read, flipped over the first page, seconds later put both pages down. 'Inspector Clark has laid an official complaint concerning you. You are charged with disobedience of rules, insolently questioning his authority, and bringing the division into disrepute. Offhand, I'd say these charges cover most of the misfeasances of which a DC is capable.'

There was a brief silence.

'Has it ever occurred to you that an order from a senior officer is only given after careful consideration of all known circumstances?'

'Sir, when a young girl is kidnapped—'

'Whom you failed to identify as a relative, as required by the rules. You then ignored the inspector's orders to stay clear of the investigation into the possible kidnapping and questioned someone whom you knew could possibly provide evidence. Finally, in a burst of mistaken enthusiasm, you trespassed on the suspect's land in the middle of the night and were found there. It's difficult to distinguish between the stupidity of your intention and the stupidity of your execution.'

'Sir, someone has to believe it more important to find Elaine than to worry about rules.'

'You are saying a search of Morning Farm had to be

made, even when in the inspector's judgment there was insufficient evidence to apply for a search warrant?'

'There is sufficient evidence.'

'You judge the inspector's interpretation of the facts to be wrong because you lack the emotional stability to view them dispassionately. I agree with him, much as I would like to disagree.' Perry's surprise was observed by Woolley. 'You make the mistake, Constable, of believing your senior officers are either unable to appreciate, or are indifferent to, the evil the missing girl may be suffering.'

'Maybe not indifferent, but not prepared to risk their careers.'

'As Inspector Clark has mentioned, you have a pointed tongue. We are bound by the law, not sentiment; were it otherwise, there would be no law.'

'But there might be justice.'

'And as much or more injustice. We are doing everything possible to find your niece; everything the law allows us to do, that is.'

'Then she won't be found until it's too late.'

Woolley put the papers back in the briefcase. 'You appreciate the seriousness of the charges Inspector Clark has made?'

'Yes, sir,' Perry said sullenly.

'And the only justification for your actions would be that you can show you have been right from the beginning?'

'How am I supposed to do that when I've been thrown off the case?'

'A question to which I have given some thought. Since your record until now has been good and it is clear your attitude and behaviour has been due to emotional distress and not bloody-mindedness, I have decided that for once expediency should be accepted. I am going to suggest to Inspector Clark that his complaint be put on ice, you be accepted back on the case, and Burrell again be asked for permission to search his property.'

'He'll refuse.'

'Of course. However, such a request will provide reason for several officers to walk across the land since they believe permission will be granted and wish to set to work immediately. While walking, someone might find a trace or an article which proves Elaine Oakley has recently been on the land – naturally, should that happen, one would hope it is not you who finds it since, given the circumstances, there might be questions regarding whether the find was genuine. It might be another thread from her frock, but that is very unlikely. Perhaps something small and loose, like a bracelet, a watch, a hairband. One can only speculate and hope.'

'Sir . . .'

'Well?'

'The moment Burrell sees several lads crossing his land—'

'Inspector Clark will take a long time persuading Burrell to reverse his refusal to allow us to search.'

'I've repeatedly been told we can't go on to the farm without a search warrant, but you're saying . . .'

'You will not be searching, merely wandering across the land, waiting for orders.' Woolley paused. 'It will be in your interests, Constable, to learn to appreciate the subtlety of the indirect.' He put the clipped papers back in his briefcase. 'The granting of a search warrant by a magistrate may well be our last chance to find Elaine in time. I hope to God you find success.'

Sixteen

'It's bloody impossible,' Clark said furiously.

'What's up, sir?' Yates asked, as he stood in front of the desk.

'The superintendent has told me to take Perry back on the case.'

He was too surprised to observe his customary caution in the face of a senior. 'That can't be what he meant?'

'You think I suffer from delusions? "And take Perry," he said, "with several others to ask Burrows for permission to make a search."'

'But that has to be a waste of time.'

'I know that, you know that, even Stone may know that, but our detective superintendent doesn't. Take Perry back on the case? When he buggered everything up yesterday? When he thinks orders are a laugh and rules are fodder for the karsy? The super's lost his grip.'

'Best not to forget something, sir.'

'What?'

'He has the reputation of being a crafty old . . . a crafty operator. D'you think he could be giving those orders because of some reason that's not immediately obvious?'

Clark was annoyed he had allowed his feelings to become obvious. 'Haven't you any work in hand?'

'More than enough, sir.'

'Then would it be an idea to start doing it?'

*   *   *

'Well?' Sandra said tightly as Perry entered the house.

'I'm not out on my neck.'

'Thank God! I've been dreading . . .'

He held her tightly for a short while. 'The superintendent gave me a low-key blasting, then said he was telling the guv'nor I was to return to the case.'

'The superintendent can't be the ogre people have called him.'

'I'm damned if I can make him out.'

'Don't bother. Love, I'm feeling sick from relief.'

'Can I get you something?'

'A stiff drink.'

He laughed. 'I was thinking in terms of medicine.'

'If only we had some champagne, I could float on the bubbles.'

Later, when they were in the sitting room, she said, 'Something's still wrong, isn't it? You're worried. Is there something you haven't told me? Is there still the chance of trouble?'

'Only if I do something really crazy.'

'After what happened at the farm, you're not going to do that!'

'I'm puzzled.'

'In what way?'

'Whether I was being encouraged to do that something.'

'What and by whom?'

He drank. As he lowered the glass, the ice cubes clinked against the glass. 'Woolley suggested my actions, however far off the level, might be condoned if it became obvious I had been right from the beginning. He then went on to say, in a very roundabout way, that he agreed Elaine was being held on the farm, but that on the available evidence, the inspector was right and a search warrant would not be issued. So there could be little hope for Elaine unless . . .

'He suggested some of us went with Clark to the farm

and while he took as much time as possible trying to persuade Burrell to give his permission for a search, the rest of us could conduct an unofficial one in the hopes of finding something that would be identified as Ellie's and would provide the final proof needed to obtain a warrant. He very carefully underlined that the most telling evidence would be something Ellie often wore and was likely to be lost – a necklace, a hairband.'

'Isn't that just common sense?'

'Yes. But he then added that if something were found, it would be better if I did not make the discovery because it might make people think.'

'Think what?'

'That I'd planted it.'

'No one could think you'd do a thing like that when it would be so contrary to you.'

'Finally, he said he hoped to God I found success. Why say something so odd?'

'What's so strange about that?'

'You don't normally find success; you are successful, achieve success, are lucky . . . It may be me being crazy, but I gained the impression he was suggesting I arrange for an important clue to be found by someone else.'

'How on earth could you do that?'

'Isn't it obvious?'

'Only if you're saying he suggested you did plant the evidence.'

'I am.'

'But that would be a criminal offence.'

'Doubly so for a policeman.'

'Then it is you being crazy. No one in his position would ever tell you to do such a thing.'

'The point is, he didn't.'

'What on earth are you saying now?'

'There was no specific suggestion, but when I left the

room I was convinced he had been telling me the only chance of saving Elaine was for fresh evidence to be found and since I was so desperate, it was up to me to provide that.'

'It was only an impression.'

'But a very strong one.'

'Impressions can be totally false.'

'Or spot on.'

'For God's sake, this time be sensible.'

'If I can help save her . . .?'

'If you're caught, then what happens? If you're sent to prison, how will that affect Moira and me?'

'Why presume I will be caught?'

'You were yesterday morning.'

'That was bad luck.'

'And how do you guarantee good luck this time? By burning joss sticks?'

'Sandy, you've supported me all the way so far . . .'

'But not now,' she said shrilly.

Perry parked in front of Tippens Cottage. The pocket-handkerchief lawn was still uncut and the rose bed filled with weeds. As he approached the front door, Elizabeth opened it and stared at him, afraid to ask, desperate to know. Toby rushed out barking, demanding attention.

'Sorry, Liz, there's no news.'

'She's dead.'

'There's no reason to—'

'Don't tell me you believe she's still alive. And what if she is? What will he be doing to her? Ever imagined what that could be? I do, all the time. I wish I was dead.'

Faced yet again with the dilemma of trying to lighten her misery without offering false hope, he remained silent as he followed her into the sitting room.

She sat, stared listlessly at the far wall.

'I have to check on something, Liz. It's not a new lead, just to get confirmation. So is it all right if I go up to her room?'

She did not respond.

He climbed the stairs and went into Elaine's bedroom. There was dust everywhere. One of the photographs of her on a horse had fallen backwards; the corner of a horse poster had broken free; half a sheet of crumpled paper lay on the carpet by the bed.

He crossed to the chest of drawers and opened the top drawer in which he remembered, when Elizabeth had been checking the clothes, seeing several brightly coloured hair-bands. He picked up one whose twisted blues made it easily recognizable. He looked down as he held it. Could material record fingerprints? It was difficult for anyone but an expert to keep up with the advances in identifying prints. Perhaps he had already committed his first mistake by not wearing a glove. Yet the relationship would always provide reason for his having touched the hairband . . . Unless he was more careful, Sandra would have good reason for fearing his failure.

Tuesday brought a sudden and sharp end to the fine weather. The dark clouds suggested the rain would continue and probably become heavy. The men gathered in the front room, looking as discontented as they felt.

The duty sergeant was a humorist. 'Don't forget your umbrellas.'

One of the PCs suggested what he would be happy to do with his.

Clark entered, briefly stared at Perry with angry annoy-ance. 'Are all present?'

'Yes, sir,' said the senior PC.

'Where's Sergeant Yates?'

No one answered.

'When I'm told everyone is present, I expect that to be fact.'

'I didn't know . . .' began the senior PC.

'We're not wasting time listening to what you don't know.'

The men accepted the inspector was in a filthy mood and the morning would prove even more miserable than expected.

Yates hurried into the front room. 'Sorry about this, sir. Something cropped up at the last moment.'

'It didn't occur to you to inform me of the fact?'

'There wasn't the chance . . .'

'I suggest, more accurately, the inclination.' Clark addressed the group. 'You all know what has to be done. Without conducting a search, you are to look for any trace which might be relevant to proving Elaine has recently been on the land of Morning Farm. Is that clear?'

'Not quite, sir,' said one of the PCs.

'Why not?'

'If we aren't conducting a search, how can we hope to find anything?'

'By using a little intelligence. An official search is carried out systematically; you will give the impression of wandering down to the house, uninterested in what's around you, but you will carry out a sharp visual search on the way.'

'Still don't get what it's all about,' someone muttered.

Any more than Clark did, Perry thought. He could feel the hairband in his trouser pocket. This provoked thoughts of the lined face of a bewigged judge, long since removed by position from normal life, slowly, carefully, authoritatively telling the jury that they were there to judge the facts of the case, not weigh the emotional stress the accused claimed to have suffered. The law had to be observed by all, whatever their beliefs, thoughts, emotions. In this case, fear could not be an excuse . . .

'Get moving.'

They drove to Morning Farm in a car and the van normally used for securing those prisoners arrested in the streets or during a raid. Perry sat facing a PC who chewed gum with the same unthinking rhythm of a cow chewing the cud. The bovine nature perversely annoyed him because the other had so little to worry about. The nearer they got to Morning Farm, the more likely failure became. The hairband had to be planted where it would be found and without drawing attention to himself. The earth would be spongy after the rain and the hairband could be heeled in and would look as if it had been there for the necessary length of time, but how to make certain it was secure, yet not too deep to be invisible?

'Sarge,' someone asked, 'why are we doing this?'

'Ask the super, not me. And if you still can't understand, you won't be alone.'

'If the poor kid did drop something, won't the bastard have had a look around to make certain everywhere's clear and he'll have found it? And even if she did and he didn't, it might have come from before she disappeared and was just visiting, seeing as they knew each other.'

'Likely.'

'Then we are wasting our time.'

'Where's the moan when you're getting paid to waste it?'

'It's raining so hard, maybe the second flood's started.'

'He's worried his make-up isn't waterproof,' someone else said.

The usual banter on the way to a job. Childish jokes and insults which helped to pass the time. For Perry, time raced and yet loitered. The hole in his trouser pocket was to allow him to drop the hairband unseen. But what if it became caught? Free it by shaking his leg and the facetious comments could become accusatory ones . . .

Car and van parked. Clark left the car and walked down to the house, to the accompaniment of the Rottweiler's snarling barks. They watched him hammer on the door. Burrell appeared, gesticulated angrily and stamped his way back into the house, followed by Clark. The outside door was shut.

'Move,' Yates ordered.

As they walked down the gentle slope, their efforts to appear to be casually meandering would hardly have deceived anyone.

Perry had chosen to be close to the gravel drive, on the right-hand side. The grass and weeds which should have been cut some long time ago were entwined and provided cover; the clay had many small pockets of water. He came to a stop, sneezed.

'Once a wish, twice a kiss,' the man next to him called out.

'And three times, a bloody bad cold,' was added by someone else.

He parted his mackintosh to reach into his trouser pocket. Was it in bullfighting that there was the moment of truth? Right now, he was facing the bull which had been enraged and weakened by the banderilleros, muleta held low, sword high and hilt at the chin, aimed at the 'cross' on the shoulder, the pathway to the heart with no bone to block it . . . He moved a handkerchief to let the hairband slide through the hole and down his leg, over his shoe and into the grass and weeds. He brought out the handkerchief and blew his nose, continued walking down the slight slope.

They grouped around the north side of the first Dutch barn, to the fury of the Rottweiler, taking advantage of the little cover from the growing wind and rain this offered. Yates waited a couple of minutes, but when Clark did not come out of the house, ordered them back to the vehicles. They again spread out over the ground.

Minutes later, Carlton, an older PC in sight of imposed retirement to which he did not look forward because it would mean spending so much of the day in the company of his wife, stopped, bent down, and pulled the hairband out of the grass and weeds. The line had halted and the man next to him asked him what he had found. He answered that, covered in mud, it was difficult to identify but it was some sort of material. The line resumed its slow walk.

Clark, followed by Burrell, stepped out of the house.

'What's going on?' Burrell demanded furiously. 'You're bleeding searching my land!'

'Of course not,' Clark answered.

'You think I can't see; I'm blind?'

'It's just the lads moving around to keep warm and dry whilst they wait to find out what's happening.'

'What are they doing here?'

'I was hoping I could persuade you to allow us to make a search; having them out of the vehicles would have saved time and trouble.'

'Get 'em off me land!'

'Back to the vehicles,' Clark called out.

The men crossed the grass to the drive.

'You'll be hearing from my solicitors,' Burrell said furiously.

'Sorry you think that's necessary since my sergeant will confirm that no search was to be made without your permission.'

'They was all over the land!'

'You sound as if there could be something out there you're afraid they might have seen?'

'Course there ain't nothing.'

'Then you'll agree no harm's been done.'

'You ain't no right to search.'

'Which is why, since you have refused to give your permission, there has not been one.'

Clark's suave politeness nonplussed Burrell.

'I'm returning to the station. If you think about what I said to you in the house, I hope you'll realize it has to be in your interest to grant us permission to make a search of the farm. Inevitably, your refusal makes one wonder if you have some reason for this. So if you change your mind, get in touch with me and we will quickly carry out a search which won't disturb you at all and will be an asset since it will confirm your innocence and there'll be no need to trouble you any further.'

'You come back here and I'll have the law on you.'

'As you will.'

When Clark reached the vehicles, Yates reported to him. 'Sinclair found something that could be important, sir.'

'What?'

He brought the dirt-stained material out of a forensic exhibit bag. 'It was partly in the ground, some four feet from the path. Looks like a hairband to me.'

Clark studied it. 'Where's Perry?' he finally asked.

Yates shouted across to the small group around the van and called Perry across.

'Does your niece wear hairbands?' Clark asked him.

'Why d'you ask, sir?'

'Just answer the question.'

'She does some of the time. Her mother says they suit her, she's not so sure.'

'Do you recognize this?' Clark took the exhibits bag from Yates, handed it over.

'The plastic makes it a little difficult to be certain, but right now I'd say it was hers and that I've seen her wearing it recently.'

'How recently?'

'Not long before she disappeared. Could even have been the previous day. Where was it found?'

'By the side of the gravel path.'

'Where it might easily have fallen off.' He looked at the hairband again, then at Clark. 'This is proof she's very recently been here. When he got her out of the car, perhaps she managed to break free, but he caught her and in the struggle it came off.'

'It is proof of nothing unless and until your sister recognizes it,' Clark snapped. 'Even then, it can't say exactly when or why it fell off. But maybe it'll just tip the balance to persuade a magistrate.'

Back at divisional HQ, Perry stepped into Yates's room. 'Have you got that hairband, Sarge?'

'Yes.'

'Give it to me and I'll take it to show to my sister.'

'Sit down.'

'We need to get things moving quickly. If she identifies it, a magistrate can immediately be asked to issue a warrant—'

Yates interrupted him. 'What's going on?'

'How d'you mean?'

'You make an illegal search of the farm at night, against all orders, and get shafted. Inspector Clark goes ballistic when he's told what's happened and reports you to Superintendent Woolley. That should mean an official investigation into your conduct and a likely verdict that the force can do without someone who ignores orders, makes a fool of himself and a laughing stock of the division. Only it seems that this time it doesn't mean anything of the sort. The superintendent says you're back on the case and the inspector is to take you and a number of lads along to Morning Farm to carry out a covert search . . . So I'll say again, what's going on, why have you been brought back in to the case?'

'Can't rightly say. '

'I reckon you'd sound more honest if you said you won't.'

'Straight, Sarge, I don't know any more than he told me. That he was holding me on the job because I knew Elaine and often saw her which meant I could maybe identify something as important, when no one else would consider it to be so.'

'You think he didn't reckon that if an object was found, it could be returned to the station and you could be called back from home to ask if you'd anything to say about it?'

'As I've just explained—'

'You know where the hairband was found, don't you?'

'Only very roughly.'

'Would you like to explain why you didn't notice it on the way down to the house?'

'Why should I have done?'

'On the way back to the road, it was found exactly where you were when you stopped to blow your nose going down.'

'Why d'you reckon it was like that?'

'Because I've eyes in my head and years of dealing with coppers who think they're a sight smarter than they are.'

'If you're right, it's pure coincidence.'

'Now why didn't I expect you to say that?' Yates asked sarcastically. He leaned forward, rested his forearms on the desk. His voice became harsh. 'You planted that hairband.'

'That's utterly ridiculous. What on earth makes you think I could ever do a thing like that?'

'Cut the crap. You planted it, which makes you guilty of trying to pervert the course of justice.'

'That's a lousy thing to say when you haven't a shred of proof . . .'

'When someone commits a crime, there's always proof, the problem is finding it. But there's no problem here. If you asked your sister for one of Elaine's hairbands, she'll remember; if you took it without asking, to keep her out of any chance of trouble, she'll remember when you had the chance to nick it. The man in the search line next to you likely saw something which didn't mean anything to him at the time, but will when he's asked to remember. I will testify that the hairband was found precisely in the spot where you halted on the way down and made a great show of blowing your nose to explain why you'd stopped. That you were caught on Burrell's land two nights ago is proof of the lengths you're ready to go to to land him.'

'That's nothing but circumstantial imagination.'

'Which is why you're going to take off your boots right here and now and give them to me.'

'Do what?'

'Are you now pleading deafness as well as plain stupidity?'

'You expect me to walk around in my socks for the rest of my turn?'

'You'll have a pair of shoes or trainers in your locker.'

'You've no right—'

'I don't take instructions about rights from a bent copper. Take those boots off and hand them over.'

'You're calling me bent before you've any proof?'

'For me, you're so bent you could gnaw your ass. Take 'em off.'

'You're crazy.'

'Just sickened.'

'The boots won't tell you anything.'

'They will tell Forensics, who can't stop reminding us that when one object touches another it always leaves traces. You pressed the headband down into the ground with your boot so there'll be traces from it on the boot; Forensics will find them and nail you.'

Perry felt as if he had swallowed ice. Yates was correct. There had to be the probability that on the bottom of his right boot would be a trace from the headband, proving contact. Why, he asked himself with useless impotence, hadn't he thought to clean the sole of both boots . . .? There was just the one chance of avoiding disaster. 'You're moving into deep water, Sarge.'

'I'm a good swimmer.'

'Not in this sea. So if you like life quiet, back off.'

'Well, well!' Yates said slowly. 'So when I reckoned the superintendent was playing his own game, I was dead right. And for once you did as your superior wanted, which means that for you, it's all gone pear-shaped.' He leaned forward. 'Now a word of advice to you. If Elaine is not found despite what you did, I'm handing the boots to Forensics and making a full statement. Don't rely on him coming to your rescue; don't think he'll do anything to help. He'll have covered himself tighter than an oyster in its shell and if you accuse him of leading you on, he'll leave you hanging out to dry . . . I don't make a fuss about how I feel, but I've been in the force a long time and I'm very proud of it and what it does; so proud that I hate the guts of anyone who plays it false without an overwhelming reason. So let's be having your boots.'

Perry did not move.

'Your boots. Or do I have to order a couple of blokes to pull 'em off you?'

Seventeen

Perry, parked outside home, stared through the windscreen, noting nothing because his mind raced. A walking man waved a hullo and was ignored. A child on a bicycle lost control and zigzagged across the road in the face of an oncoming car. He knew neither concern nor relief as the driver avoided the child.

Yates had virtually said that if Elaine were found on the farm, he would be in the clear; no statement would be made, the boots would be handed back. If she were not, there would be a criminal charge of trying to pervert the course of justice. Yates had a great respect for the law, but, unlike Clark, did not accept it should be held sacrosanct. Which was why he had offered him the possibility of escaping the consequences of his actions.

The chance or the certainty because she would be found? Certainty was a fool's foolishness. What if he had misread many of the vital facts which had led to his conviction that Burrell was guilty of kidnapping Elaine? . . . He hadn't misread them and Elaine was being held somewhere on the farm, unless . . . He believed he could accurately judge Burrell's character because of what he had learned, yet, as Clark had so scornfully pointed out, he was no psychiatrist. Burrell might have raped Elaine and then killed her, driven her body tens of miles away to conceal it so that she would only be found by chance. Perhaps sufficiently long afterwards that arrest and conviction became impossible . . . He forced his mind into a more positive mode.

Elaine was still alive and Burrell would be prolonging her life in order to feed his perverted desires. Since there was every reason now to believe a search warrant would be granted, she would be found.

Where was she being held? He had previously considered the house and dismissed the idea, but was there the possibility of a priest's hole? Not very likely because the house was too insignificant and would a peasant farmer have been prepared to risk his life by hiding a priest? Nevertheless, the search for one must be made. A cell dug in one of the fields? Too easily remarked, especially as one could not frequently cross land without leaving visual evidence of that fact.

He once more convinced himself she was in a cell under one of the barns. The first was filled with hay. The change in colour clearly distinguished between this year's crop and last year's. Since hay was made in early summer, the bottom bales of hay had been there before Elizabeth and Elaine had moved into Tippens Cottage, so Burrell had not yet met Elaine. The cell was not under the hay. The second barn had been empty, giving Burrell time to dig out the cell before the sheaves of wheat would be stacked to cover all traces; sheaves easily moved to allow ingress and egress, then replaced.

Perry stepped out of the car, locked it. He walked along the pavement, turned into the front garden, unlocked the front door, entered the house.

Moira hurried into the hall. 'Have you got something for me?'

'Such as?'

'The new game we saw on the telly.'

'It's only for older children.'

'Why?'

'It's rather a grown-up kind of game.' He hung up his mackintosh.

'That's stupid'

'Most of life is.'

She thought for a moment. 'Did you buy me some Mars bars?'

'I'm afraid not.'

'Why?'

'You have enough sweets as it is.'

'No I don't. You should have bought me something.'

'When it's not your birthday?'

'I'm reading a book where the daddy is always bringing his children presents.'

'A fairy story.'

'It's nice being spoiled.'

'The more frequently you are, the less you appreciate it.'

'You do say odd things.'

Sandra came out of the kitchen. 'What happened? What kind of a day has it been?' she asked in a rush of words.

'A rollercoaster. Some things have gone well, some haven't.'

She turned to Moira. 'Love, will you be very kind and go into the kitchen and watch the saucepan to see what's in it doesn't boil over?'

Moira hurried into the kitchen, proud to be asked to help with the cooking.

Sandra led the way into the sitting room. 'I try to keep her well away from all that's going on because she gets so upset without knowing why. What's not gone well?'

'A draft of us drove to the farm and while Clark went into the house and tried to persuade Burrell to give his permission to allow us to make a search of the place, we made an unofficial one of the approach to the house. We found a hairband.'

'It was Elaine's?'

'Yes.'

'You had to ask Elizabeth if it was? Can one begin to imagine what that was like for her? How can life go on and on being so terribly cruel?'

'I didn't have to ask Liz.'

'Then how can you be so certain?' she asked, sounding bitchy when it was worry which provoked her.

'Because I took it from her bedroom.'

'Oh my God! Does that mean . . . you've done what you promised not to?'

'I never promised.'

'No. But you knew how desperately I . . . What was the real motive? You could prove yourself right and everyone else wrong?'

'That's unfair.'

'Yes,' she said slowly, 'bloody unfair. You couldn't think like that. It's me talking wildly. But couldn't you see, however selfish it sounds, your first duty was to your own family? Do you know what I've been doing? Desperately hoping over and over you had given up the idea. But . . . but it's done. It worked?'

He said nothing.

'Did it . . . did it go all right?'

'It seemed to.'

'What's that mean? Tell me what happened if you don't want me to go crazy.'

'Everything went smoothly until we were back at the station. Then Yates had me in his room and accused me of planting the hairband.'

'How could he know what you did?'

'He put two and two together.'

'Then—' She stopped as Moira hurried into the room.

'It's boiling really hard and nearly going over the side,' Moira said.

'I'll be along in a moment, sweet. Just turn the ring off.'

'You've got to come now.' She took hold of Sandra's hand.

Sandra looked at her husband, her expression asking the question.

'No, he isn't going to blow the whistle,' he said.

She left, pulled along by Moira.

Wouldn't blow the whistle provided Elaine was found as a consequence of what he had done. And fear was now making him question yet again the certainties which had propelled his actions.

It was early morning. Clark, dressed with extra care because the magistrate he had spoken to believed clothes maketh man, stepped into Yates's room. 'We've got it.'

'Without much trouble, sir?'

'All that really concerned him was being woken up – as he put it – in the middle of the night. Everything ready?'

'Give it a quarter of an hour, sir.'

'Why?'

'The architect isn't here yet.'

'Ring his place and find out where the hell he's got to. You have the phone number?'

'No, but I can easily—'

'It's to be hoped you've organized the rest of the operation better than this.'

Yates silently said all the things he would have liked to say aloud, crossed to the internal phone and asked the duty sergeant to look up the number in the local list. When given it, he dialled on the outside phone.

The call was answered by a woman whose high-pitched voice and strangulated vowels suggested to him a long, horsy face and buck teeth. Her husband had driven from home a quarter of an hour before; there had been absolutely no need to ring to find out if he had left. If he said he would do something, he did it. He was not like so many people today who could never be bothered . . .

Will no one rid me of this ghastly woman? he wondered, as he patiently listened. He finally replaced the receiver. When a day began badly it often never recovered.

Eighteen

The two cars and van drove into the yard, to be greeted audibly by the Rottweiler. Burrell stepped out of the house and shouted at the police to clear off.

Clark crossed the litter-strewn gravel, came to a stop in front of the house. 'Mr Stan Burrell?'

'Bloody King Kong.'

'Is this Morning Farm?'

'Buckingham Palace. I'm going to get you lot for harassment.'

'I have a—'

'I don't give a toss. I ain't seen the kid since I left her by the field. If you won't leave me alone—'

'I have a warrant entitling me to search your house and land.'

'Shove it up your jacksy.'

'If you try to restrain us, you will be arrested.'

'I'm ringing my solicitor.'

'He will inform you that you cannot prevent us making this search.'

'What are you looking for?'

'Elaine Oakley.'

'Haven't I said a hundred times, I ain't seen her?'

'We have reason to believe you are holding her captive. We will search your house now.'

Clark called Yates across. 'Mr Gosling and two hands in the house, the rest to search the outbuildings and the land.'

Clark led the way into the small hall. 'Is there a cellar?' he asked Burrell.

'Of course there ain't.'

'Are any of the rooms locked?'

'Didn't know you lot was coming.'

Clark turned to Gosling, a thirty-year-old architect who looked a forty-year-old one because of advanced baldness and a heavily lined face. 'Where do we start?'

'A look at the outside.'

'You think she's hanging up in a cage?' Burrell sneered.

Once outside, Gosling withdrew a length of tape from the leather-covered measure in his right hand, handed the brass-protected end to Clark. 'We'll measure all four walls and comparison with inside figures will show if there's any discrepancy.'

Before they measured the northern wall, Gosling stepped back and looked up.

'The chancellor is still left with one tax he can impose on us.' Noticing Clark's expression, he added, 'That indentation in the brickwork almost certainly denotes a window that was bricked up at the time of the window tax. There might be a very small room hidden by the blocking, but I rather doubt that.'

The outside measuring completed, they went inside. 'Where's the trap door to the loft?' Gosling asked.

'There isn't one,' Burrell muttered.

'No trap door or no loft?' Gosling said lightly, refusing to be riled by the other's boorishness.

There was a bathroom and three upstairs bedrooms, each heavily beamed, two with fireplaces. With the help of Clark, Gosling took measurements which he compared with the outside ones. 'Allowing for the standard size brickwork of a house of this age, there's no missing space.'

'Maybe you reckoned there'd be a banqueting hall?' Burrell sneered.

'The blocked window,' Gosling continued, 'was, as I thought, merely an honest Englishman's objection to paying still more tax to keep the politicians in clover. We'll have a look at the loft now.'

The trapdoor was not readily visible because it had been carefully placed between two beams and covered with the white plasterboard that matched that elsewhere on the ceiling.

'We need some steps,' Clark said.

Burrell muttered something, left. He returned with a five foot stepladder.

Gosling set the stepladder, climbed high enough to lift the trapdoor, then two more rungs to be able visually to search the loft with the aid of a torch. 'Nothing here,' he said, his voice slightly distorted, 'except for a lovely king beam.'

Clark briefly tried to remember what a king beam looked like.

They returned downstairs. Gosling checked the massive central fireplaces in the dining and sitting rooms, which served the central chimney, declared them free of any hidden space. The ground floor was clean.

'Not found anything, has you, like I said you wouldn't?' Burrell sneered. 'But telling you blokes anything is like talking to a brick wall.'

Clark and Gosling went outside, Gosling crossed to his car and drove off. Clark walked past the barns and looked out across the fields. The searchers were almost up to the copse that bordered the field at the far end. He opened a broken-down gate and walked across the stubble. A rabbit bolted when he was within six feet of it and made for the nearest hedge, its ears laid back, its white scut bobbing.

Yates was in the middle of the line of searchers and he called a halt as Clark approached.

'Nothing?' Clark asked.

'Less than that, sir.'

'Take the wood carefully.'

'I've told them to halt before the slightest disturbance in the undergrowth; there's a good covering of old leaves to record anything.'

The coppice was no more than a hundred yards deep and four hundred wide. Within yards of the road there were considerable signs of movement and while it was probable this had been caused by people stepping off the road into the coppice for one reason or another, the area had to be closely searched. Nothing of any consequence was found.

They returned to the yard to be met by Burrell who, when told what was about to happen, shouted, 'You're going to do what?'

'As I've just said, empty out the corn.'

'You bleeding don't.'

'We have the right to search where we wish.'

'You think she's hiding in the wheat?'

'Being held captive under it.'

'Like she was hiding in a secret room in the house?'

Clark turned and called out, 'Shift the corn as fast as you like.'

They were eager to carry out the order, convinced they must soon find Elaine. Two men climbed up on to the sheaves. One of them picked up a sheaf by the binder twine and went to throw it over the side, misjudged the swing because the sheaf made for awkward handling, and it landed back on the stack, only a couple of feet from where he stood. There were cheers and jeers.

'Sir,' Perry said.

'What?' Clark snapped, infuriated by incompetence.

'They need to use pitchforks.'

'Then find some.'

Perry crossed to where Burrell stood. 'Where do you keep the pitchforks?'

'Ain't got any.'

'Next thing, you'll be telling me you've given them all away since I helped you load.'

'You was wasting your time then and you're wasting it now. She ain't under the wheat or anywhere else around here.'

'Then why so nervous?'

'I ain't.'

Burrell did seem to be relaxed, but that could merely mean he was able to conceal his emotions. Perry walked over to the nearest outbuilding, in a lesser state of disrepair than the others, opened the door with some effort because the hinges were rusty. Against the right-hand wall, points on the ground, were four pitchforks. He chose the two with longest handles and carried them across to the barn. As he handed up the first one, he advised, 'Use them with curve upwards.'

'Listen to old Farmer Giles,' someone said. Yet again, weak humour was being used to ease tension.

After initial difficulties, the two PCs gained sufficient proficiency in unloading the sheaves and before long they were down to the footing row. The watchers became silent and many began to move uneasily around, finding that preferable to standing still.

The last sheaf was thrown aside. 'What are you waiting for?' Yates shouted excitedly.

The men hurried to form a line and then slowly, carefully searched through the litter of broken stalks and chaff, using boots and occasionally hands, to check the hard-packed land. They reached the far end, having found nothing. Men swore.

'Go back over it,' Clark called out. 'Search more carefully.'

Their return took almost twice as long, but the result was the same. The ground was unbroken.

'Didn't I say?' Burrell demanded. 'Why don't you empty the other barn so as I can claim compensation for that as well?'

Nineteen

Perry, wishing he were somewhere, anywhere, else, parked outside Tippens Cottage. Despite his attempt to conceal his optimism the last time he had visited Elizabeth, it was quite possible she had sensed it. If so, she would be hoping, expecting he would tell her Elaine was safe.

She was drunk. She listened to his faltering admission that they had failed to find Elaine and poured herself another whisky. She added water, most of which ended outside the glass. He used a cloth from the kitchen to mop this up.

'Whatever happens, Liz, you mustn't give up hope,' he said, knowing how impotent and useless his exhortation must be. With no further leads to follow, only luck would now save Elaine and luck had deserted them.

'He doesn't know,' she said suddenly, slurring her words.

'Who doesn't know?'

'He doesn't know or he would have come here.'

'Who are you talking about?'

'Ray.'

He had not heard her mention her husband from the moment Elaine had disappeared.

'He would be here,' she said a second time.

'Liz, the news has been in all the papers and on the television. He must know what's happened.'

'You only say that because you dislike him so.'

Both he and his father had disliked Ray from the day she had introduced him to them.

'He used to play with Elaine.' She began to weep.

He felt even more helpless now than at any time since the Wednesday she had phoned to tell him Elaine was missing and he had confirmed the fact.

'If I hadn't come here to live, she wouldn't be dead.'

A policeman met hundreds more 'ifs' than did most. If I hadn't had a row with her. If she'd gone to the shops the usual way. If he'd had one less drink . . .

'Why?' she suddenly said violently.

Why me? The question asked by every victim.

She finished her drink, reached for the bottle.

'Hadn't you better give it a rest, Liz?'

She poured a drink, added very little water, this time without spilling any.

Probably she was right, he thought. Drunkenness provided a brief respite from memories – or at least from acknowledging their consequences.

She spoke quietly. 'You met us in Carnford. Just me and Elaine. Ray was working. Elaine was wearing the pink frock she liked so much because it had a horse on the front. She was so excited on the way down, I had to stop the car so she could go behind a bush. When you left before we did, to return to work, she said how she loved her uncle Ronald. She will never call you Ron. It always has to be Ronald. Did you realize that?'

'No,' he answered thickly.

'She skipped all over the house and didn't mind it would be so much smaller than home; said it would be such fun to live out of town.' Elizabeth used a handkerchief to wipe tears from her cheeks. 'I told her that before we went home, I'd drive around so we could see what the countryside was like. We went all over the place and then when we were coming back, she said she was hungry, so I bought some chocolate in the little shop in the village. Then we saw Blacky in the field and she asked me to stop so she could give him the chocolate she had left. As she was giving it to him, he drove up in a van and got out to find out what was going on, started talking to her. Of course, I went over to them. He looked rough, but seemed pleasant. We talked a bit and I mentioned we'd be moving in as soon as builders finished the work on the house.'

'You're talking about Burrell?'

She took no notice of his question, drank. 'Not long before he cleared off with that bitch, Ray was talking about buying an Aston Martin. Always lived in the clouds. I suppose she believed he was serious and that's why she went off with him. I've always hoped he discovered she was as big a liar as he and she hadn't any money, even though she behaved as if she were a millionaire. She was older than him . . .'

'Liz, please forget him and think very carefully. Did you both meet Burrell for the first time on the day you came down to look at the house before you bought it?'

'What's that matter?'

'You've always said you first met him after you'd moved here.'

She drank.

'It could be vitally important.'

'What could be?'

'The time you first met Burrell.'

'It was when Ellie fed Blacky chocolate.'

'And that was before you bought this house and moved down here?'

'I keep telling you.' She emptied her glass. 'I always tried to watch her riding and jumping Blacky. She was so good I thought she could maybe become a champion showjumper when she grew up. But she's not going to because she's dead. And I wish to God I was as well.' She sobbed.

Sandra poured gazpacho from a carton into two soup plates.

'Liz was tight?'

'By the time I left, very much so,' Perry answered.

'Too blotto to make sense?' She picked up one plate and handed it to him as he sat at the kitchen table, picked up the other and put it down for herself.

'Sense enough for me to learn she and Elaine first met Burrell when they came down to look at the house and decide whether or not to buy it.'

'You sound as if that's important?'

'Until now, I've always understood they didn't meet him until after they'd moved in.'

'How does that make any difference?'

'It gave him time . . .'

'I'm asking if it will make a scrap of difference to what's going to happen to you?'

He had just filled his spoon; he held it above the plate. 'No.'

'So it's still the same – because Elaine wasn't found, Yates is going to report you?'

'Yes.'

'Won't anyone understand why you did what you did?'

'There's nothing to understand as far as authority is concerned. I planted the evidence, full stop.'

'But it was at Mr Woolley's suggestion.'

'Yates has convinced me that if the accusation is put to him, he'll express bitter shock that anyone could believe him capable of such a thing.'

'You were trying to save Elaine.'

'In law, results cannot justify the means.'

'You must tell—'

'Love, if I could present a recording of his saying to me what he did, he'd no doubt explain it away by saying he was merely presenting a hypothetical possibility and had no idea I might be so naive as to believe he was suggesting I carry it out.'

'Then you're . . .' She did not finish.

'I had to do it. For Elaine's sake, I had to take the risk.'

'No, you didn't.' She abruptly stood. Her voice was high. 'You didn't have to destroy our future.' She hurried out of the kitchen and upstairs.

He had lost her support. The fact heightened his misery, but did not surprise him.

The sun returned on Thursday, along with puffballs of cumulus. Perry parked his car, went into the building and up to the fourth floor. Fuller and Stone were in the general room. Fuller said, 'Sodding bad luck, not finding her.'

Final bad luck.

'And to add to the misery, the skipper's shouting for you.'

Perry had reached his desk. He stared down at the left-hand corner where an unknown DC had carved, with considerable skill, a small skull. The sculptor could have had no idea how his work could become so very apposite.

'Stub a toe,' Stone said.

He nodded his thanks, left. The door of the sergeant's room was half open and he entered. 'You've been shouting for me, Sarge?'

'Shut the door,' Yates said.

He shut it.

'I've something to say. Not easy, but it needs to be said. When we started unloading the corn, I found myself praying for the first time in years; praying we were going to find her. The prayers didn't work, of course. But you'd given me the hope to pray, which was more than the law had. You follow?'

'I think so, Sarge,' he answered uncertainly.

'There's my key.' He brought it out of his coat pocket and put it down on the desk.

'The key to what?'

'To my locker.'

'Are you saying . . .?'

'Not saying anything except return the key as quick as you like.'

Perry stepped forward and picked it up. 'I . . . I won't forget this.'

'You will if you don't want to land both of us in the deep end.'

He went down to the locker room, which was empty. He inserted the key in Yates's locker, opened the door, brought out two black bin liners.

Seven minutes later, he dialled home on the mobile. 'It's me. The sarge isn't going to say anything to anyone.'

There was a long silence, then Sandra said, 'Again, slowly.'

He repeated what he had said.

There was a longer silence. 'Oh my God! . . . Are you sure?'

'He's given me back my boots. The nightmare's over.'

'I . . . I don't know what to do.'

'Indulge in a woman's cure-all and have a good cry.'

He walked to the Four Ducks. When on duty, he normally never had a drink, but it would have taken superhuman restraint not to have something alcoholic this day. He ordered a gin and tonic. He had just been handed a glass and paid when Young George came up to where he stood.

'Still waking up people in the middle of the night to ask daft questions?'

'When I can, but I don't get the opportunity as often as I'd like.'

'Bloody sadist!' Young George called across to the bartender and asked for a pint of bitter. 'Not found the girl?'

'No.'

'Poor little kid. You know how to stop all those bastards? Bring back hanging.'

'Probably wouldn't prevent them; certainly not when their desires are beyond their control.'

'You sound like one of those poofters in parliament. Wait 'til one of them has a daughter raped and murdered and see how soon they change the law.'

'If they're poofters, they're unlikely to have daughters.'

'Bloody smart, except when it comes to doing your job.' Young George drained his glass. 'Let's be having yours.'

'Thanks, but I've not finished.'

'You drink like a kid who's not yet off his mother's titties.' He turned, elbowed his way through to the bar, returned with glass refilled. 'You need help.'

'If you've learned anything or heard any whispers that might help us find her, I need to know.'

'I ain't heard anything; what I'm saying is, you tell me what to do and I'll do it.'

It was a time for a diplomatic answer. 'I'm really sorry, but—'

'Look, Mr Perry, it don't matter what you want, if I can do it, it's done.'

'It's good to hear you say that, but there really is nothing.'

'Then you let me know if things change.'

'I certainly will.'

There was a call to tell Perry his lunch was ready. He went through to the small room in which were six tables, four of them occupied. He sat and buttered a slice of baguette. The waitress, who also served behind the bar, brought him the shepherd's pie he'd ordered. He ate. He remembered how strange, even eerie, Young George's scrapyard had looked at night with forms not sharply edged and shadows creating dangers. And how mixed had been Young George's judgment of Burrell. A man who was so slack he had let his farm become a dump. But a man who knew how to haggle with the devil; the previous winter hay had been in short supply, but he'd managed to buy some at so low a price, it was if he had mesmerized the seller . . .

Perry hurried into the CID general room. 'Any idea where the skipper or the guv'nor is?'

'Both with the great white chief,' Gough answered.

'They've gone up to county HQ?'

'The super's here, in the guv'nor's room as far as I know. And from the look of him, it's gales.'

'I need a word with him.'

'Stay well clear.'

'Can't.'

'Why not?'

'A man has to do what a man has to do.'

'More bloody fool him for having to do it.'

Perry left, walked along the corridor. An 'engaged' sign was illuminated above the inspector's door. He knocked. There was no response. He knocked again.

'What the devil is it?' Clark shouted.

Perry opened the door and stepped inside.

'Are you blind?'

'Sir, it's very important. I now know for certain where Elaine's being held.'

'How do you know?' Woolley, seated to the side of the desk, demanded.

'I was talking to my sister when she told me that she and Elaine met Burrell last November; until now, I've always understood they did not do so until this May.'

'Why is that significant?'

'In November, she mentioned they would be moving into Tippens Cottage, which means he knew Elaine would soon be living in the neighbourhood, so he had time to plan. When I learned that, I remembered that soon after

Elaine went missing, I spoke to someone who told me that during the last winter, Burrell had bought hay for his stock. Yet on his farm, last year's hay is still in the second Dutch barn, which raises the question, why, when he's so careful with money, did he buy what he didn't need?

'The answer has to be the obvious one: he needed feed for his stock yet to leave last year's hay stored to make it seem the floor of the barn could not have been disturbed for two seasons. Believing Burrell had not met Elaine before May of this year, one accepted he could not have planned to kidnap her before then; therefore, if he had dug out a cell, it could not be under the old hay.'

'And now?'

'I don't quite understand what you mean, sir?'

'Are you about to suggest we unload the hay in order to search underneath it?'

'We have to.'

'You assured us the girl was under the corn; could not have been more certain. So we unloaded it. No cell. The result? Burrell, through his solicitor, alleges police harassment and in support of his claim cites the many times you questioned him despite his constant assertions of total innocence; your trespass on his land at night; the police raid in which his harvest of corn was so badly mishandled and damaged, it cannot be sold for thatching. In addition to involving the blood-sucking lawyers, he's spoken to a television reporter who, he claims, will put out a report on screen and that will, as always, be biased heavily against the police.

'So once more, the police are going to be presented as a fascist organization which takes no notice of an individual's rights.'

'Someone has to get hold of the TV people and make them understand that we had to do what we did in the hope of saving a girl's life.'

'You are naive enough to imagine they will accept that, will forgo the opportunity to pillory authority? The chief constable compares our handling of the case with a performance by the Keystone Kops.'

'Elaine is imprisoned under the hay.'

'And now you suggest we apply for another search warrant?'

'Yes, sir.'

'Have you considered how the magistrate to whom the application is made will react, knowing that if the second search proves equally unsuccessful, the police will become the target of every uninformed critic and, inevitably, he will be drawn into the smear?'

'The public must be made to realize—'

'You appear intent on brainwashing the entire population. The public realizes what the media wishes it to.'

'But—'

'There will be no second incompetent disaster.'

'Fear of suffering a loss of reputation is so very much more important than saving a girl's life?'

'You have an unfortunately direct manner,' Woolley said slowly, 'as I think I have said before. If I were not prepared to accept you are solely motivated by emotion, I would consider you insolent.'

'We have to search under the hay.'

'If – when – there is the hard proof that to do so will offer a reasonable chance of rescuing the girl, that order will be given.'

'I've just told you—'

'Only that Burrell first saw the girl earlier than previously thought and he bought hay when it appeared he had no need to do so.'

'You can't see what that means?'

'You are asking me to accept that this time you are right, despite the fact that last time you were hopelessly wrong;

that I should ignore the risk of further publicity highly detrimental to the force.'

'I say again, is that more important than a girl's life?'

'A question that only arises when one can be certain there is at least a reasonable chance Elaine is confined under the hay.'

'You refuse to see that what I've told you proves it's not a reasonable chance, it's a certainty?'

'That's enough,' Clark snapped.

Woolley said calmly, 'Perry, you should have served long enough to accept that there are times when politics are present to curse everything they touch. Here, we have a political problem as well as a human one. I cannot ignore the first, much as I wish to; emotion can have no place in this investigation.'

'But—'

'I need to remind you we still have no proof, hard proof, that Burrell is guilty of kidnapping Elaine Oakley; merely a series of facts which can appear to provide proof when lumped together, but are of insufficient account when viewed separately? What you have told us today merely adds two more facts. That you were so certain she was under the wheat when she was not proves how fatal it is to draw assumptions from ambiguous facts.'

'We know she was on the farm because of the hair-band.'

'That proved sufficient for the magistrate, but in court even a clueless counsel would show there could be no significance in Elaine's undated presence on the farm since Mrs Oakley had expressed her trust in Burrell by letting him bring Elaine back from school in his van; what more natural than that she should visit his farm?'

'Why would he have bought hay the previous year when he had more than enough for his stock?'

'A question easily answered. Were the coming winter a

very sharp one, with prolonged snow and ice, his own hay would not be sufficient to feed the stock. Being a wise man, he therefore bought extra as an insurance.'

'There would have been enough for the stock he has, however prolonged the weather.'

'You are a farmer as well as a policeman?'

'No, sir.'

'Then your opinion can only be of small moment.'

'He's a man who'll never pay for anything which he isn't convinced he will need.'

'That is pure conjecture.'

'Why did he buy all the extra tinned food, bread, chocolate . . .' Perry began heatedly.

'I am not prepared to discuss every aspect of the case.'

Perry managed to speak more calmly. 'Sir, Burrell kidnapped Elaine and has been holding her in a cell that was dug out after his perverted imagination was triggered by learning she would soon be moving into the neighbourhood. He covered the cell with bales of old hay in order—'

'Constable, let me say quite clearly that if I am provided with one piece of evidence which proves beyond any reasonable doubt Burrell is guilty, I will give orders to make the search. Until then, this will not happen. Do you understand?'

'Yes, sir.' Perry hesitated, turned and walked over to the door.

'And perhaps it needs to be pointed out that any such evidence must be uncovered in circumstances which provide no chance of Burrell's claiming it has been introduced by an overenthusiastic policeman.'

One had to admire the chief superintendent's devious nature. Perry opened the door and left.

Twenty

Sandra walked into the sitting room, a glass of whisky in her hand. 'This is because Moira says you're all gloom again and need cheering up.'

He took the glass from her. 'My daughter has all the right ideas. Aren't you going to have one?'

'No.' She handed him the glass. 'Why are they all so blind?' She settled on the arm of his chair, rested her forearm on his shoulder.

'For some, it has become more than finding a missing girl. It's the political question of managing to save, or rather, not lose, rank.'

'It's inhuman, barbaric to think like that.'

'If they believed that what I have been saying is right, they wouldn't; all the time they can find reason to think me wrong, they will.'

He drove to Tippens Cottage. As he braked to a stop behind a small red car, a man stepped out of the front door. He said goodbye to Elizabeth, walked the few feet to the road, smiled a hullo at Perry, climbed into the car and drove off.

Elizabeth, who'd had Toby in her arms, put him down on the ground, remained standing in the doorway. Toby rushed to greet Perry and did his best to get in the way as he went forward and kissed her on the cheek. 'Wasn't that the vicar?'

'Here, as he put it, to comfort me in my hour of need.' She spoke with increasing bitterness. 'Hour of need? Days of living hell.'

She had never been able to find relief in acceptance.

'Have you learned anything?'

'Unfortunately, no.'

She bent down to pick up Toby who, with terrier playfulness, carefully kept out of reach. 'Come here,' she ordered, with sudden, sharp anger. He slunk up to her, tail down. She picked him up. 'I told the vicar I prayed Elaine was dead and he was appalled; insisted I mustn't pray for evil; God's mercy would return her to me. His mercy let her be kidnapped, so why should He suddenly go into reverse? Can you tell me that?'

'No.'

'Do you want a drink?'

'If it's not too early.'

'Makes you sound as if you're thinking of wearing a dog collar.'

'I would find it too tight for comfort. A gin and tonic, please.'

'Are we going to go on standing here?'

He followed her indoors, went into the sitting room as she continued into the kitchen. He looked around the room. The signs of neglect were more obvious than before.

She returned, handed him a glass, sat. 'Ray still hasn't been in touch. Perhaps he's ill and the bitch won't help him. More than likely since she's only time for herself. Did you know I'd met her?'

'I didn't.'

'In Harrods. The food department. I'd been looking at the tins of gourmet soup, turned round, and there she was with Ray. He spluttered, she wobbled her double chin and talked like someone in a hag mag. Said she was so sorry about what had happened, but when she'd met him, there'd been electricity between them. Should have electrocuted the bitch.' She stroked Toby. 'It's an odd world, isn't it?'

'Too odd to understand.'

'And where ignorance is bliss, 'tis folly to be wise. Who wrote that?'

'It's a proverb.'

'Ray and Elaine had such fun together. Yet he just cleared off with the bitch . . . Could you go off with another woman and leave Moira and Sandra?'

'No.'

'Did you ever wonder why Ray really left me for her?'

'You've said he thought her to be very wealthy.'

'It was more than money.' She stood. 'Give me your glass.'

'No, thanks.'

'Your collar getting too tight?'

She left, returned with her own glass refilled, sat. Toby jumped on to her lap. 'I know I've always said it was because he thought she was rolling in money, but it was more than that. I wouldn't cooperate in bed.'

'Best forgotten.'

'I suppose he got his ideas from magazines. The bitch may be older than he, but much more willing than ever I was. Perhaps she was in a sharp set before she looked like a worn-out grandmother. Like I said, it's a strange world. Because of sex, I had Elaine; because of sex, I've lost Elaine.' She cried as she drank.

Perry unlocked the front door and stepped into the hall. Moira came out of the sitting room and greeted him, called out to Sandra that he was home.

He went into the kitchen. 'Sorry I'm once again late. I had to stay on longer than I wanted.'

Moira entered. 'Daddy needs a drink.'

Perry smiled. 'I think not this time, though thank you very much for suggesting that.'

'Moira,' Sandra said, 'would you like to help me and lay the table?'

'No.'

'Yes please.'

'Why can't Daddy do it?'

'Because he's been very busy and needs to relax. Into the dining room with you, put out everything in the right order on the table and don't forget the serving spoons.'

She stamped her way out of the kitchen.

Sandra bent down and opened the oven door. 'I turned the thermostat down, so it's not going to be too bad. How was Liz?'

'The local vicar called and she told him she prayed Elaine was dead.'

'That's a terrible thing to say to anyone, let alone a vicar.'

'Not so terrible if one understands that she can't stop thinking what Elaine might be suffering and how death could be a mercy.'

'Did you tell her that you may have learned something?'

'When it would only raise her hopes which could all too easily be dashed again because the top brass are as thick as lead?'

'I wasn't thinking. Is she still drinking heavily?'

'She had a couple of whiskies while I was there and they obviously weren't the first, but she was in control.'

'Can't she see that drinking heavily won't change anything? She ought to . . . Who the hell am I to talk like that? Nothing's easier or meaner than to advise and criticize someone who's in pain when one isn't.' She put a saucepan of water on to boil. 'I didn't want to start the vegetables before you returned. The beans won't take long.'

Moira hurried into the kitchen. 'I've laid the table perfectly and I'm so hungry, it hurts. I think I need some chocolate to ease the pain.'

'A slice of bread and butter will be far more effective.'

'If I starve to death, it'll be your fault.'

'I think that's unlikely, remembering the enormous breakfast you had.'

'Breakfasts don't count.' Moira left.

'We ought to be grateful she eats instead of trying to look like a matchstick,' Sandra said, 'but if she's not careful, she'll start to put on weight . . . How did things go?'

'Woolley was down from county HQ and at the station. He won't listen to me, refuses to do anything unless hard proof turns up. And where the hell can that come from now?'

'Something has to be done.'

'Knowing that isn't going to make it happen.'

Twenty-One

Fuller, followed by Perry, entered Yates's room.

'Don't hurry, there's all the time in the world,' Yates said, with his usual primitive sarcasm.

'Sorry, Sarge, but I had a call from a snout,' Fuller said.

'Useful?'

'No.'

'And you?' he asked Perry. 'You were having a chat with the chief constable?'

'I gathered you wanted to see the two of us together, Sarge. Didn't like to waste your time saying the same thing twice.'

'I waste my time whenever I try to get you moving. There's a report just in of a team of dippers working the town's supermarkets. According to one store detective, it's two men, one woman, which means the first man barges into the victim and while he's apologizing, the woman with her small fingers nicks the purse or wallet and hands it to number three who's out of the building before chummy realizes he's been bankrupted.'

'How long do we have to be out there?' Fuller asked.

'Feeling tired already? You're out until you're called back for something more important. You've a problem with that?'

'Some of the stores are open all night.'

'Then it looks like you have a long time ahead of you.'

'But I've a sharp date this evening . . .'

'If she's lucky, you won't be making it.'

They returned to the general room to close down the work they had been doing.

Their initial sharpness had faded and they were suffering from the policeman's constant complaint – boredom.

As Perry watched an argument between two women, one large, one small, but both vociferous following a collision of trolleys, his personal mobile rang. He brought it out of his coat, opened it, raised it to his ear.

'There's still more bad news,' Sandra said, her voice shaking. 'Elizabeth tried to commit suicide. She was found and rushed to Carnford General. They can't yet tell me how seriously ill she is.'

'I'll get there right away.'

'I hope . . . Have we done anything but hope for days?'

He replaced the mobile in his pocket, hurried to where Fuller was staring with interest at a couple of young women in short, short skirts.

'Cover for me, Jack. I've got to skive.'

'You reckon I'm going to help you enjoy yourself when I'm likely to miss out with Susie?'

'My sister has just been rushed to hospital.'

'Sorry, mate. You clear off and I'll cover. If the sarge turns up, I'll say you're in one of the other stores and then give you the buzz.'

They had both come in the CID car, but Perry's need was greater than Fuller's so he drove it across town to the newly built Carnford General, which looked rather like a prison and had had a cost overrun of hundreds of thousands.

He used his authority as a DC to overcome bureaucratic obstruction to a visit outside visitors' hours and soon was in a ward of eight beds; Elizabeth was in the end one, behind a curtain screen. He sat by the side of the bed, shocked by her appearance. He reached out and put a hand on her shoulder, felt her tremble. When life knocked one down to the floor, he thought, it then gained further pleasure by kicking one.

After a while she murmured, 'I just couldn't take any more. The desperate hoping, the prayers that failed, the terrible thoughts filling my head; then a man rang. He said he had Ellie and thought I'd like to know what was happening to her. He told me what he'd done. I screamed at him to let her go free. He laughed and said it was much too soon to do that because he was going to have more fun . . .'

'He was lying, Liz. He was one of those bastards who gain enjoyment from knowing the pain and terror his words cause.'

Either she had not heard him or did not believe him. 'When he said he was going to find out if a man really could . . . It was too much. I had to escape . . . Then I woke up and hadn't escaped, had to know Ellie was still being abominably brutalized. Oh, God, why wasn't I left to die?'

'You have to understand. The man was lying from the beginning.'

'How can you say?'

'Because I know that type of man.' Impossible to tell her Elaine was imprisoned under the hay at Morning Farm but authority blindly refused to find and release her.

'He told me she was wearing her blue dress before he took it off. How could he know what she was wearing unless he had kidnapped her?'

'The television and papers reported what she was wearing. He learned from them.'

'He said she was wearing pink knickers.'

'You told me they were white, but I didn't pass that on to the media. He was making that up to terrify you even more.' She had not mentioned Elaine's underwear when describing how she had been dressed, but he had to try to help her out of her misery.

He again said the phone call had been a hoax; she again was unable to believe him. He tried to ease a little of her misery with the promise he would hurry to Tippens Cottage and make certain Toby was all right. She seemed indifferent to Toby's well-being.

After saying goodbye, having promised to return as soon as possible, he left her; on his way out, he spoke to the ward sister.

'Can you tell me what the prognosis is?'

'The doctor doesn't think there will be any permanent damage.'

'Thank God for that! But I'm worried my sister is so depressed she might try to commit suicide again.'

'We're taking very great care to make certain that doesn't happen, Mr Perry.' She hesitated. 'The doctor did say it might prove difficult to help her out of her deeply distressed state of mind.'

'Or impossible?'

'I am not qualified to answer.'

Yet he judged she was certain that unless circumstances changed, Elizabeth would, on her release from hospital, probably try to kill herself again.

Perry's police mobile rang. He answered the call.

'Where are you?' The speaker was Yates.

'Tesco, Sarge.'

'Anything happening?'

'As calm as a millpond.'

'There've been no reports from other stores so the mob likely sussed you or have moved on. You can come back and do some work.'

Before leaving the car park, he phoned Sandra. 'It's Ron. The doctor doesn't think there's any permanent physical damage. The breaking point was the sod of a man who rang her and claimed he'd kidnapped Ellie and described in revolting terms what he had done to her and what he was going to do. I tried to make Liz understand he hadn't had anything to do with her disappearance and was just gaining pleasure from terrifying her, but she couldn't believe me . . . The doctor reckons it may well be difficult to draw her out of her suicidal misery.'

'How can anyone expect her to when all the time she's thinking of what's happening to Ellie? You've got to find her or there'll be two lives lost.'

He said goodbye, replaced the mobile in his pocket and stared through the windscreen at the lines of parked cars. For a detective, failure to clear up a case was a familiar occurrence. There might not be enough evidence to identify the guilty man or woman; there might be enough for that, but too little evidence to justify arrest; the trial might bring out some small error in law of no consequence to the question of guilt, yet which resulted in the accused being discharged; the jury might reach a not guilty verdict which was bereft of logic. Yet in the face of failure, a detective could tell himself the criminal had gone free because someone else was a silly sod and there was no reason to blame himself. Very occasionally there was a failure when a man found it all but impossible to release himself from blame.

He found the heavy doors open and walked into the junkyard. In daylight, the scene was not eerie, merely one of demolition and decay.

'What's it this time?' Young George demanded as he stepped out of the office. 'Are the Crown Jewels missing?'

'I need help.'

'Then you've come to the wrong place. Help a bloke what comes in the middle of the night, wakes me up and falsely accuses me of having a ton of coke?'

'In the pub, you offered to do anything that would help Elaine.'

'That was the beer talking.'

'You won't help save her from hell?'

'What's wrong with you lot doing your job?'

'That's a long story. It's act now or it's too late.'

'I'm not understanding.'

'Do you have a tractor that works?'

'And if I have?'

'Does it have a fore-loader?'

'When I put one on.'

'I want to borrow it.'

Young George stared at Perry. 'One of us is round the twist.'

'Can't you understand I'm trying to get you to help me save Elaine Oakley?'

'By borrowing a tractor?'

'And a fore-loader.'

'You don't want a baler as well?' He turned to go back into the office.

'I obviously made a bad mistake back in the pub. I forgot that talk's easy and beery talk is even easier.'

Young George turned and walked forward until three feet from Perry. 'There's some talk that ain't easy. Which is why I don't shout that my kid sister was grabbed by a man who mucked around with her. I'd of put the noose around his neck and kicked the trapdoor open. I'd do the same to any of the bastards.'

'Then lend me your tractor and I'll find Elaine.'

'Is this talking straight?' he asked slowly.

'I can't talk any straighter.'

'What's the tractor for?'

'Elaine is being held in a cell under a barn full of bales of hay; some of them have to be moved.'

'Your blokes too tired to do that?'

'No one else believes she's there.'

Young George put his hands in the pockets of his overalls, turned to his right and walked over to an ancient immobile Austin, returned. 'Ever used a tractor?'

'Yes.'

'Unloading bales?'

'No.'

'Then you'd be no bloody use.'

'I'll manage.'

'You won't. I'll do the unloading.'

'Impossible. There could be trouble.'

'You think you're the only man big enough to meet it?'

Twenty-Two

'Stub your toe,' Sandra said in a tremulous voice as Perry approached the front door.

'Why say that?' he asked sharply.

'Isn't that what you people say to someone who's heading into trouble?'

'Why imagine I'm doing that?'

'Because you're such a poor liar. Because I know you're not off to the station to clear up some work.'

'The DI said he wanted me—'

'To keep right away from Elaine's case.'

'I have to check something at the station.'

'Love, you'll never win a prize for lying. You know what sickening horrors Ellie is suffering; you're frustrated because no one will believe what you say; and since you're convinced you know where Ellie is, you're determined to save her whatever the consequences.'

He did not continue to deny that. 'I have to do it. But you mustn't worry.'

'I'll be worried sick. But I'm not going to try to stop you this time because you have to act. So stub your toe bloody hard.'

He left. It was the need to save Elaine which forced him forward; it was courage which prevented Sandra's trying to hold him back.

He drove to Pearce Wood, turned into The Cut and, avoiding when he could the larger overhanging branches or thicker clumps of weeds and brambles, continued down the gentle slope until certain the car was well hidden from the road.

He climbed out, picked up from the front passenger seat a torch and the can of CS gas 'borrowed' from stores. He walked the short distance to the corner of the wood, pressed the light switch on his watch. Fifteen minutes to midnight. Excitement, tension, nervousness had brought him there too early.

The night sky was clear and the moon frequently hidden. In some ways an advantage; in others, a disadvantage. His mind raced. If the worst came to the worst, of what could Young George be found guilty? Trespass with a tractor? In itself, not a crime. Malicious damage? The twine of some of the bales might part and the contents spill out, the hay dispersed, not damaged. Only a pedantic lawyer would call that anything other than very minor damage. But he was risking not only his career, but prison. Despite having returned his boots, Yates might consider he had been taken for a fool and reactivate the charge of his planting the hair-band and there could just be sufficient circumstantial evidence to convince and convict. He wished this operation was just wild imagination . . . He was becoming a coward. Had he not condemned his seniors for refusing to act outside the law's boundaries?

A car stopped twenty yards from where he waited and he had the sudden fear that Yates or Clark had discovered what was happening. Common sense returned when he realized the driver was relieving himself. How could Yates or Clark have known he was there?

Midnight. He stepped out on to the road and walked quickly, now there was no room for doubt or fear.

As he neared Morning Farm, he heard the booming exhaust of the approaching tractor. It turned the corner and headlights briefly lit up him and the entrance to Morning

Farm. Young George braked to a halt and he climbed on to the rear axle, held on to the rear wings as they moved forward. *Iacta alea est*. The only Latin he remembered from Caesar's *Commentaries*, which he had once had to try to study. The die is cast.

Light reached past the empty barn and lit up the second one filled with hay. The Rottweiler, snarling, barking, strained at its chain. As the tractor came to a stop, Perry jumped down on to the ground. 'Start on the far end facing the house and go in to the depth of a couple of bales,' he shouted. It was an unnecessary order since he had, before they had left and much to Young George's impatient annoyance, detailed what they were to do more than once.

Young George drove the tractor in a half turn, raised the hydraulic arms and went forward to dig the spines of the fore-loader into one of the top bales.

Clark was sleeping soundly, snoring unmusically, when his wife shook him awake. 'What's up?' he mumbled.

'Can't you hear the phone?' she asked.

'No.'

'The house could fall down and you wouldn't know it. Aren't you going to answer it?'

As he rolled out of bed, put on a pair of slippers, and went downstairs, he wondered bitterly why they were always saying they must have an extension phone upstairs in the bedroom, yet never arranged for one to be installed. He crossed to the small table on which the telephone stood, lifted the receiver. 'Yes?'

'It's Sergeant Yates, sir.'

'So what the hell has got you ringing at this godforsaken hour?'

'Burrell has just reported that Perry is attacking the hay in his barn with a tractor.'

Clark stared at the framed print which he disliked, but his wife cherished.

'Sir, did you hear . . .'

'I believe it.'

The bright outside lights on the farmhouse were switched on, and the front door opened. Burrell stepped out, a twelve-bore in his hands. 'Clear off or I'll blast you to hell!' he shouted.

Perry walked forward. 'Then you'll spend even longer in prison than you've already chalked up for yourself.'

Burrell came down the steps and, keeping the gun aimed at Perry, crossed to the Rottweiler. 'If you ain't out of here in one minute, I'm letting him loose.'

'Don't be stupid.'

'You've bleeding asked for it.' He released the chain.

The Rottweiler did not rush, but, crouching slightly, moved forward slowly, like a lion stalking its prey.

'Get him!' Burrell shouted wildly.

Encouraged, the dog rushed forward.

Perry pressed the release button on the can of gas in his right hand. The dog came to a sudden stop and whimpered as it tried to ease the pain in its eyes by brushing its head against the side of its leg.

'Put the gun down.'

Slowly, Burrell leaned over and placed the gun on the ground.

'Step back ten paces.'

He stepped back.

Perry went forward, picked up the gun, broke it and extracted the two cartridges which he pocketed. 'On the ground, face downwards, your hands behind your back.'

When Burrell was lying down, he used plastic restraints to secure Burrell's wrists and ankles.

The bales had been stacked in traditional fashion: the bottom layer end on, the next sideways, the third end on, and so on. Young George had unloaded to a depth of two bales down to the second layer from the bottom. Success was close; but no closer than failure.

Perry watched one bale dumped with the other loose ones, then the tractor made a half circle and moved forward to dig the tines into the next bale. As this was lifted, thick boarding, resting on the bales on either side, was revealed. He pointed. Young George nodded and then very slowly, very carefully, removed the bales around the boarding except for those on which it rested. Perry tried to lift it, but found it too heavy. Young George left the tractor and went over to help him.

Perry switched on his torch. The cell was six feet square and deep. Elaine, her auburn hair in a tangle, face stained with dirt that traced past tears, blue dress dishevelled, crouched in fear.

'It's Uncle Ronald,' Perry said hoarsely.

She seemed unable to understand.

'Ellie, it's Uncle Ronald. We've come to save you.'

She stared up, desperately hoping but as yet not willing to believe.

Perry turned to ask Young George to find a ladder; the other had already left to do so.

'We're getting a ladder, Ellie, and you'll be out of there in no time.'

'Where . . . where is he?' she asked shrilly.

'He's on the ground and trussed up like a chicken to make certain he can't move. He'll never again hurt you.'

Young George returned with a short ladder which he passed across. Perry dropped the end to the bottom of the cell, then climbed down. As he stepped clear of it, keeping his head low, Elaine suddenly escaped her trance and threw herself at him and gripped him with all her strength.

He climbed the ladder, using one hand to support her,

the other himself. He stepped free and went to put her down on the ground, but immediately she resisted, tightening her legs around his waist. One-handed, he brought the mobile out of his pocket and dialled the station. 'PC Perry here . . .'

'Man, if you don't want to be hanged, drawn, quartered, and then beheaded, take off for Outer Mongolia.'

'I've found Elaine. An ambulance to Morning Farm, priority.'

He returned the mobile to his pocket, crossed to his car where he persuaded Elaine to release him and sit on the front passenger seat. He settled behind the wheel and she nestled against him.

An ambulance arrived. A female doctor carried Elaine into the back of this and closed the doors. As she did so, two cars drove up, their headlights adding light to the scene. Yates and Clark were in the first, four PCs in the second.

'What state is she in?' Clark demanded.

'Scared silly, but no obvious signs of physical injury that I could see, sir,' Perry answered.

'She was being held in a cell under the hay?'

'Yes.'

'You've been down into it?'

'Only to bring her out.'

Clark ordered Burrell to be picked up and placed in the rear of one of the police cars and to be closely guarded. As this was done, Woolley drove into the yard, hastily left his car and spoke to Clark.

'The girl's in the ambulance with a woman doctor, sir, and Burrell is secured in the Rover, under the guard of a PC.'

He listened to the rest of the DI's report in silence, turned and spoke to Perry. 'It seems you were right after all and we were wrong.'

'Yes, sir.'

'And determined to prove that!'

Perry kept a tactful silence. Clark had scorned his judgment of Burrell's character and motives because he was no psychologist, but he'd been right.

'Did you have any trouble with Burrell?'

'Just had to persuade him not to shoot us, sir, and to teach his dog not to bite.'

'Has he suffered injuries which we'll explain were caused by his resisting arrest?'

'No, sir.'

'For once, you acted with discretion?'

Perry gained the impression this had been a mistake.

The rear doors of the ambulance opened, the doctor climbed down and crossed to where they stood. 'Thankfully, there seems to be no physical trauma. Of course, it will take time to evaluate any mental damage.'

'You're saying she wasn't raped?' Woolley asked, surprised.

'After all she's been through and from what she told me, I deemed it unnecessary and unwise to carry out a physical examination since I am convinced that she was not.'

'Then what happened?'

'Each time he went down into the cell, he made her take off what she was wearing, then stared at her whilst he fiddled with himself. Fortunately for her, never with success.'

'Bloody hell!' Clark exclaimed. Then hurriedly, with old-fashioned manners, added, 'I'm sorry.'

'There's no need to be,' she replied briskly. 'I was just as astonished and relieved.' She spoke to Perry. 'I understand Elaine's mother is your sister?'

'Yes,' he answered.

'It's in the child's best interest for you to get her back

with her mother as soon as possible and leave all questions for another time.' She spoke to Woolley. 'You agree?'

'It's your judgment, Doctor.'

'Then you have it.' She addressed Perry again. 'Explain to your sister that as soon as reasonable, Elaine needs to be examined by a psychologist to determine what, if any, lasting effects she has suffered from the ordeal and how best to deal with them.'

'Unfortunately, Elizabeth is in hospital after attempting suicide because of the impossible stress of believing Elaine was either dead or suffering agonies.'

'Then they need to be together at the first possible moment. Which hospital is your sister in?'

'Carnford General.'

'I'll arrange for you and Elaine to see your sister immediately, despite its being so late.'

Moments later, Perry and Elaine drove away. Woolley watched the tail lights turn right on to the road, spoke to Clark. 'You'll have to agree there are advantages to having under one's command an officer who is arrogantly incapable of observing the law, following the rules, or obeying orders.'

Clark muttered something which might, or might not, have signified his agreement.

The ward was in half-darkness. Those patients who were awake, watched with the interest of boredom as a nurse, Elaine, and Perry entered. Elaine raced forward and threw herself on to her mother.

Once before, Perry had seen an expression similar to that now on Elizabeth's face. It was when Sandra had given birth and first looked at Moira.

Twenty-Three

There was a small television set in the kitchen which allowed Perry to watch the news before he left to go to work. As he ate the first slice of buttered toast and marmalade, there was a report from a government spokesman. Public transport had been greatly improved, education had taken a great leap forward, hospital lists had fallen . . . He wondered if Carnford was the only town in the country where public transport was still largely invisible; two of the three state schools had been heavily criticized for the poor level of education they offered; and reputedly if one suffered from a kidney stone, it would have become a rock before it was treated.

The presenter turned to a fresh subject. 'It has been reported that Elaine Oakley, who disappeared eleven days ago, has been found . . .'

'Sandy,' he called out.

She hurried into the kitchen. 'What's up?'

He pointed at the screen.

'. . . is said to be in good health. Her mother, who is in hospital, told our reporter that she was too overcome with joy and relief to give an interview. A hospital spokesperson said that both mother and daughter were progressing well.'

As Sandra sat on a kitchen chair, Clark appeared on the screen.

'Inspector, you were in charge of the investigation into the disappearance of Elaine?'

'That's right.'

'May we all congratulate you on bringing it to a successful conclusion.'

'Thank you.'

'Would I be right in thinking that the moment when you found Elaine means far more to you than any congratulations or praise?'

'I can only say it was the most wonderful moment possible.'

'One can imagine that . . . Would you call the investigation a difficult one?'

'Very difficult. But I had the advantage of having a first-class team of officers who carried out my wishes without any hesitation and we were finally successful in saving the unfortunate girl.'

'Can you explain how you managed to find Elaine, Inspector?'

'There was very little evidence, but there were possibilities which had to be judged as to their possible relevance. This is when, as I have always held, imagination becomes important. There is merit in imagining, on the strength of what one does know for certain and a knowledge of the criminal mind, what could have happened and then carrying out the investigation on the assumption that it had. Out-guessing the criminal, I call it. Thankfully this proved very successful.'

'What do you say to Burrell when he claims you searched his farm without either his assent or legal justification?'

'There are occasionally exceptional circumstances when one has to be like Nelson – to look with a blind eye. I became convinced Elaine was held in a cell under the hay in one of the Dutch barns at Morning Farm, but unfortunately there was not sufficient proof of this to pursue the normal course. Yet since a child's life was at stake, I decided that regardless of the law, an immediate search must be made.'

'Had you been wrong and she had not been under the hay, would your actions have been condemned?'

'Very heavily.'

'Then what would have been the consequences to you?'

'My career would almost certainly have been ended.'

'Then Elaine owes her freedom – indeed, probably her life – to your readiness to ignore your own interests.'

'I suppose you could put it that way.'

Sandra said furiously, 'It was you who discovered where Ellie was because you used your imagination when no one else would; it was you who took all the risks when the inspector refused to take a single one; it was you who brought Elaine out of that hellhole when he wasn't even there! How can he be such a hypocritical liar?'

'A natural politician.'